A THOUSAND LIES

A YOUNG ADULT NOVEL

KATHY CASSEL

HPP

HPP

Haven Point Publishing, Lynn Haven, FL
A Thousand Lies
Copyright © 2022 by Kathy Cassel
Cover and Interior design: Diana L. Sharples
Cover photo: "Blue Brick Wall" by Marina Pokupcic, from Dreamstime.com

Haven Point Publishing
Lynn Haven, FL

Paperback ISBN: 979-8-9859043-4-5
Ebook ISBN: 979-8-9859043-5-2

Summary: When teen photographic artist Bailey Collins discovers all she believed of her life is a lie, uncovering the truth becomes a peril-filled quest that may bring the answers she seeks—or turn out to be the worst mistake of her life.

Keywords: Identity, personal identity, belonging, relationships, family relationships, self-discovery, runaways, teen photographers

Endorsements for A Thousand Lies

A Thousand Lies is a novel for YA readers you won't be able to put down! This exciting journey of mystery, written with Christian values, is a dramatic story with relatable characters and will keep you guessing until the end. Don't miss another wonderful adventure brought to you by author Kathy Cassel.

Kathleen Hansley
licensed independent social worker/
clinical therapist (MSW, LISW)

Filled with mystery, suspense, adventure, and teen drama, *A Thousand Lies* is a page turner that's hard to put down. With its fast-paced, intriguing plot twists, this young adult novel will not disappoint. The author writes from a Christain worldview, so parents can trust her stories, Another gem from Kathy Cassel.

Crystal Bowman
award-winning bestselling author of
more than 100 books including
I Love You to the Stars

A Thousand Lies is a young adult novel I plan to include in my middle school classroom library! This fast paced, suspenseful adventure is just the type book my students will devour. Plus, I love how the story is told form a Christian viewpoint, so I know my students are reading quality literature. Kathy Cassel is a master at writing intriguing stories that address tough topics in an age-appropriate way. I highly recommend *A Thousand Lies* to all middle and high school teachers!

Velma Hunsucker
veteran middle school teacher of 24 years

Kathy Cassel delivers yet another story packed full of intensity, discovery, and action in this thrilling book about a teen trying to uncover the secrets that encompass her. As the pieces begin to fall into place, the danger increases, making her question everything. In the process of looking for answers, she also seeks to understand herself and the world around her. Start to finish, this story will rocket you along and leave you breathless.

T.E. Bradford
author of the YA/Fantasy *Divide Series*

Dedication:

A Thousand Lies is dedicated to all those who are searching
for a place to belong.

Acknowledgments

A special thank you to Jeanette Windle, fiction coach extraordinaire. I could not write realistic YA fiction without your guidance. For every "this doesn't work," you are right there with a "but I know how to fix it." And by time the story is ready for publication, you know the characters and story as well as I do. And the books are stronger because of you.

Thank you to my husband, Rick, and to our children who believed in this book and encouraged me in the writing of it. You listen and offer suggestions from the conception of an idea through each stage of writing to the finished book. You add heart to each story.

Thank you to Diana Sharples for an excellent cover and interior design. You add the professional touch to my books.

CHAPTER ONE

I crept down the hall, willing the polished wooden floorboards not to creak, then slipped into my parents' home office. Originally a third bedroom at the far end of the hall from the other bedrooms, it's now where my parents, Tim and Patty Collins, store the paperwork for their shop, Collin's Auto Repair.

It isn't that I'm not allowed in their office. But my parents might wonder why I was in there at four a.m. Especially since I'm not a morning person. Or why I was using only my phone app for light. But I was on a mission, and I hoped the office held what I needed—family photos required for my sociology project.

Mom had said she'd find photos for me. But Dad's shop had picked up more business in the last couple years and outgrown the small building that housed it. Dad recently purchased a bigger place. Now every spare moment Mom and Dad have is spent packing up their old shop and moving into their new one.

The upside is that they'd hired me to help, so my bank account is a lot larger than it used to be. I'd been saving for a better camera, one I could use for a career in photography. So having a steady paycheck was good. The downside is that our family movie nights had been a lot fewer due to lack of free time.

More importantly right now, the photos for my sociology project were due, and I didn't have them. Okay, I had a couple photos of my grandparents Mom gave me when I first asked. But when I'd asked for young pictures of myself—as well as of her and Dad—she'd gotten upset, saying she didn't have any.

I'd already searched the kitchen drawers. Along with utensils, I'd found a variety of notes scribbled on scraps of paper, two combs, several books of matches, community theater tickets, and so on. No photos of any kind.

The family Bible hadn't yielded any pictures either, and there wasn't a photo album in sight. Which was what had led to my early morning search.

Before this project, I'd never thought about the lack of family pictures. There's an 8x10 of me on the living room wall where I'm about a year old. That's it. If it weren't for the fact that every person who sees me with Dad tells me I'm the spitting image of my father, I might wonder if the lack of pictures meant I was adopted. But it's obvious I'm not. My dark-blonde hair, almost white in my baby picture, is the same shade my dad's used to be. The bigger giveaway is the blue eyes and dimples we share. There's no denying the shared genetics.

A soft noise in the hallway alerted me that someone else was up. I clicked off my flashlight app and froze. Steps were coming toward me. I quickly dropped to the floor. Crouched out of sight behind the desk, I peeked around the corner, hoping whichever parent it was didn't notice the office door was open.

Mom padded by in bare feet, headed toward the kitchen. Then the sound of running water filled the silence, followed by that of the pot being put in the coffee maker. Of course. She'd forgotten to set the coffeemaker last night, and Dad isn't human until he's had his first cup of the day.

As soon as Mom returned to her bedroom, I turned my flashlight app back on and shone it around. Where to start? Sitting in the desk chair, I opened the central drawer. It held pens, paper clips, and other small office supplies. Sliding open the top side drawer, I found electricity and water bills.

The bottom drawer was more of the same, so I moved to the filing cabinet, a standard metal four-drawer model. The top drawer let out a sharp metallic whine when I tried to ease it open. I froze and listened. The house was still silent. Relieved, I tugged harder.

A quick search showed it was full of my old schoolwork. Everything from kindergarten stick-figure drawings to fifth grade spelling tests. The next drawers held my work from middle and high school. Had they saved every project I'd done and every test I'd taken? Still, no photos.

With a sigh, I crouched and tugged at the bottom drawer. It didn't budge. I yanked harder. Nothing. Was it stuck, or was it locked? Bracing my feet, I grasped the handle and put all my strength into it.

The filing cabinet gave a mighty shudder as the drawer opened. I barely had time to register the lock box it held before a pile of car repair manuals stacked on top of the cabinet began spilling off of it. I jumped up, trying to catch them before they hit the floor.

Too late! In the stillness, the crash sounded like an avalanche. I pushed the drawer shut, then quickly began picking up the manuals and piling them neatly back on top of the file cabinet.

Moments later, light filled the room. I shut my eyes and put my hand over them, shielding them from the brightness.

"Bailey! Whatever are you doing?"

I eased my eyes open. Mom stood in front of me in pink Winnie the Pooh pajamas, hands on hips. "I'm trying to find my baby pictures and photos of you and Dad."

"I told you there aren't any." Mom's voice held a hint of impatience. "I gave you ones of your grandparents."

"How can there not be any baby photos?"

"We had them on a thumb drive, but it got misplaced."

"No backup? No external hard drive?"

Mom gave me an exasperated look. "You know Dad and I aren't up on technology. We only started storing our invoices electronically a few years ago."

"What about prints of the photos? A family photo album?"

"I always meant to get around to it, but—"

"What do I do about my sociology project? We're supposed to be creating it in class today. I'll get a bad grade on what should be a fun assignment."

Mom sighed. "I have a smaller copy of the portrait on the wall that I can give you. I'm sure your teacher will understand. There are plenty of photos of you a bit older. I can get you those."

I studied her. Maybe it was the early hour or the news there weren't any baby pictures for my project, but my brain wasn't processing well. "I'm not adopted, right? You're not hiding the real reason there are no photos?"

Mom chuckled. "With the resemblance between you and Dad? You came along after we'd given up on having any children. You're our miracle child."

4

"I know I'm not adopted, but I thought I'd throw it out there anyway," I said, having heard the miracle child story before. "Are there any photos of you and Dad before I was born? Maybe a wedding photo? One of him in his Navy uniform?"

Mom sighed. "I can tell neither of us is going to get any more sleep. Why don't you shower and dress, and I'll make pancakes?"

I nodded and headed toward the bathroom. I showered, then dressed in jeans and a long-sleeved T-shirt before stepping into the hall. Mom was coming out of the office with three photos.

"These aren't as good as digital photos. They were taken with a film camera ages ago. But I was able to find one of our wedding day and one of Dad in uniform like you wanted."

I looked at the photo of Dad. He was certainly in uniform, but he was turned away from the camera, saluting an older man also in uniform. Only his profile was visible. I studied the wedding photo. Mom looked young in her flowing white dress, her face bright. Although I have a strong resemblance to my dad, I don't share much genetically with my mom.

The last picture was a copy of the large one on the wall. The paper and the picture itself were a better quality than the other photos. I turned it over to look for a studio trademark. Whatever had been written on the back was blacked out. "This one looks professional, but there's no studio name on it anywhere."

Mom hesitated, then answered. "It was taken by someone we used to know. She was better with a camera than Dad or me, but we haven't seen her since you were little."

"What was written on the back?"

Mom's eyes furrowed. "Could have been the date it was taken."

I nodded but doubted it. Why would someone black out a date?

I slid the pictures into a folder in my backpack, questions still filling my mind.

CHAPTER TWO

Two hours later, I stepped out the door into the morning light. On this first Thursday in May, our small northern Indiana town was finally warming up. But the spring weather could be fickle, forty degrees Fahrenheit or seventy or both in the same day. Reaching back inside the door, I grabbed my jacket.

With my camera bag over one shoulder and my backpack over the other, I waited curbside for my friend Reese Patterson. Moments later, he pulled up in his X Terra. A gift from his often absent father, it was a vehicle that served Reese's athletic nature well with plenty of room in back and racks on the top to hold sports equipment. Reese would soon turn seventeen, and I was grateful that he had a driver's license and vehicle. It saved me a boring bus ride to the only high school in our town.

Jogging to the front passenger door, I climbed in. As I buckled my seatbelt, Reese grinned at me and ordered, "Close your eyes and hold out your hand."

I looked at him quizzically.

"Just do it," he said.

I raised my eyebrows in question but did as he said.

He dropped something small and heavy into my hand. I opened my eyes. It was a perfectly made miniature compass keychain. He smiled. "For you. So if we're ever apart, you'll always be able to find your way back to me."

I grinned at his corny line. "Like we're ever more than two

school hallways apart." I studied the compass. "This is nice. Thank you."

Taking the compass from my hand, Reese attached it to the strap of my camera bag. "It seemed like the perfect thing to go on your camera bag. After all, your photography brought us together, and someday it's going to take you great places."

Warmth crept up my neck at Reese's praise though it was true photography had brought us together. Reese had moved to town last year and joined the soccer team, quickly becoming a valuable player. As yearbook photographer, I always photographed the home games. Sometimes Draya Paul, my best friend, would attend games with me. Draya was like the sister I'd always wished for and never gotten. We'd met in sixth grade and had become instant friends.

Near the end of last school year after Reese turned sixteen and acquired a driver's license, he'd invited Draya and me to ride to school with him instead of riding the bus. At first, I'd thought it was because he was drawn to Draya with her olive skin, deep brown eyes, and straight ebony hair, inherited from her mother, whose family came from Sri Lanka. We are basically opposites. She's light-brown. I'm pale and sunburn easily. She's tall and thin while I'm average height and built athletically as my dad likes to say. Besides her exotic looks, Draya has a bubbly personality and genuine warmth. But to my surprise, Reese had asked me out instead Draya.

Of course, my parents had denied permission since I wasn't yet allowed to date. Instead, they'd invited him over for dinner. Then the week after school ended, Reese and I attended adventure camp together in a nearby town, which meant a lot of shared fun. We'd been close friends ever since. In a few weeks, this school year would end, and we'd be headed back to the same camp.

Reese skillfully maneuvered to Draya's house, where she was waiting. Always stylish, she was wearing black leggings and a long purple sweater. She bounded down the steps and climbed in the car. "Morning, Bailey. Morning, Reese. Is this going to be a great day or what?"

I looked at her. "What has you so cheerful today?"

"Counting down to the end of school. What else? Next year we'll be juniors, and Reese will be a senior!" A contagious smile filled her face.

I grinned. "Of course you're counting down to the end of school. I would be too if I were going on an amazing trip to Sri Lanka."

"I don't think you'd enjoy the flights. With layovers, it's a grueling twenty-two-hour trip," Draya said. "And we are going to England as well to visit Dad's family as well as friends Mom made at university."

I knew Draya's parents had met while attending university in London. Draya's father is British and a prominent neurologist. Her mother is a computer engineer, which allows her to work from home anywhere there is internet so when Draya's father was recruited by our regional hospital complex, it was easy for her mom to transplant her work across the Atlantic. No surprise their daughter was as brainiac and good with computers as Mr. and Mrs. Paul.

Draya leaned forward. "Did you bring your pictures for the project?"

I let out an exaggerated sigh. "Well, it turns out there aren't any baby pictures of me."

I launched into the story of my four a.m. excursion into my parents' home office, embellishing it a bit to make it more interesting. Draya frowned. "All of them were lost? You'd think they'd have been saved to an external hard drive."

"For sure!" Reese interjected. "I'm more curious about the lockbox you turned up. Was it full of money or secret papers or what?"

"Didn't you hear her?" Draya demanded with a laugh. "She didn't see what was inside. And this isn't some spy show. The lockbox probably has their important documents like their marriage license and birth certificates. You know, so if the house burns down or something, the most important papers are safe."

"I suppose so," Reese agreed. "My parents keep birth certificates, social security cards, and car titles in a fireproof lockbox in their closet. Still, my idea was definitely more exciting."

I grinned. "I don't think my parents have any big secrets. The worse thing they've ever done is skip church because they were so tired from a long work week."

Draya laughed. "Well, that is a pretty serious offense in our town."

Reese pulled into the school parking lot, and the three of us headed side-by-side toward the entrance to Central High School, a two-story brick building with polished tile floors and stairs with iron railings. We each had different first period classes but would be together second period for sociology.

While the geometry teacher droned on about theorems, my mind wandered back to early morning.

Why did Mom's explanation about the photos still nag at me?

And as Reese had asked, what was in that lockbox?

CHAPTER THREE

The tinge of anxiety I'd felt going into second period without baby pictures eased as we started on our projects, working together in groups of three, using the school computers. Reese and Draya decided we should start with my collage, so we began on that, using the template provided.

The one-year-old version of me in the first photo was wearing a lavender dress and ruffled socks. The photo had been taken with me sitting on a blanket with a torn corner in the middle of a field of yellow daisies. My short, wispy hair was much lighter than my now dark-blonde hair, and my eyes were the same color as the sky. The picture looked perfect like a calendar page or an advertisement for a portrait studio.

We added the photos of my grandparents along with the photos Mom had given me this morning. The rest of my collage was made up of pictures of family hikes at a large local county park, tubing on the river that ran through it, and celebrating holidays at home. With so few pictures, my collage was quickly completed, and we went on to Draya's project. Reese and I helped her choose from the excess of photos she had, which took us to the end of the class period.

I expected the rest of the day to be routine. But in second-year photography, my final class of the day, Mr. Markenly announced a surprise end-of-year field trip. "We have an unexpected chance to visit a photography exhibit at a college in

Chicago a week from tomorrow. This is a unique experience, and students from other art classes will also be taking part in this opportunity."

I couldn't help smiling. Reese and Draya both had art electives, so we might be able to attend the field trip together. I tuned back in to what Mr. Markenly was saying. "Pick up one of the permission forms from the back table. Due to the late notice, you'll need to get it signed tonight and returned tomorrow. We only have the use of a single fairly small school district bus, so the first twenty to turn in their slips will go."

My heart sank. I wasn't sure I could get permission. When I'd wanted to attend a summer art camp and had even been offered a scholarship due to my yearbook photography, my parents had been adamant about me not going. They claimed it was because the camp was in Chicago and they were worried about crime. Seriously? I would have been at art camp, not out on the street.

I wondered what my parents would say about me going on a field trip to Chicago. I would be with our school group and wasn't likely to suffer from any inner city violence. Still, I never knew when their overprotective spirit would kick in. Sometimes I wished they'd had four or five more kids so they couldn't spend all their time worrying about me.

The driveway was empty when Reese dropped me at the curb after school, indicating that neither of my parents were home yet. I hopped out of the X Terra clutching my backpack and camera bag, then leaned back in. "Thanks again for the compass. It's perfect. See you tomorrow."

"You want me to come over to work on homework later?"

"Sure. Maybe you can convince my parents I should go on this field trip. They wouldn't let me attend art camp in Chicago last year."

Going inside, I found the family laptop on the kitchen table. Logging in, I located the website for the college hosting the art exhibit. Might as well learn something about the college before my parents arrived home.

Not an hour later, both my parents were home, and my dad was reading the permission form. "Why do you need to miss a whole day of school to look at photos in Chicago? You leave at six a.m. and don't get back until school ends. What about the classes you'll miss?"

"I can make up the work. I'll even do it ahead."

As though on cue, the doorbell rang. Hurrying to answer it, I let Reese into the house.

"By the way, Reese is going on the trip," I announced.

The look on my dad's face said he didn't care whether or not Reese was going.

"I wouldn't miss it," Reese said. "It's a great opportunity to visit the college and see what they have to offer, including scholarships."

My dad raised his eyebrows. "It's a college visit too, then?"

Reese gave his disarming grin. "It would be a wasted trip if they didn't provide a tour and tell us what the college offers, wouldn't it?"

I jumped in with my newfound knowledge. "According to their website, they have a journalism degree with a specialty in photojournalism. It's a popular major, and ninety percent of their graduates gain employment in the field. Plus they offer scholarships for outstanding ability and academic success."

Dad looked at Mom. She shrugged. Then Dad turned and studied me. His eyes, the same color of blue I saw in the mirror every morning, looked tired. His dark-blonde hair was fading to gray. He was clearly trying to do too much in both fixing cars and moving into a bigger facility. A twinge of guilt flitted through me since I knew this wasn't technically a college trip in the way I was letting Dad believe, though we'd be seeing the art building and eating in the college cafeteria.

Dad looked at the permission slip again, then sighed. "I'll sign this, but I hope you get a lot more out of this trip than merely the chance to look at pictures."

I nodded and tried hard to bite back a smile, but I couldn't. "Thanks, Dad, Mom. This is going to be great."

Although the field trip was a week away, there was little talk of anything but the trip until then. Previously, our school outings had been to a neighboring city for a community theater play or a tour of the city government building or once even sitting in on a trial. It had been a long time since a class went the three-plus hours to Chicago—and it would be a long time again if our behavior was not exemplary, Mr. Markenly informed us.

I wonder how excited I would have been had I known what lay ahead.

CHAPTER FOUR

When field trip day arrived, Reese and I sat together while Draya sat with her friend Sara in the seat across from us. The bus pulled out of the school parking lot onto a small country road winding through corn fields. Not until it reached a major highway did it feel like we were really on our way.

"My mom is so excited to visit family in Sri Lanka," Draya said.

"Do you speak Sinhala?" Sara asked.

"No. Thank goodness most people in Sri Lanka speak English, or I'd be in trouble." Draya looked around me to Reese, who was sitting next to the window. "Isn't your family going somewhere this summer?"

Reese's face hardened before he smiled an obviously forced smile. "No. Dad can't take time off for something as pointless as a vacation. Right now he's so busy preparing a presentation for the building project he's going to bid on he doesn't come home half the time."

Sitting next to Reese, I could feel the tension rising in him. "That's not right. Your family should be more important than his job."

Reese swiveled to face me. "Hey, don't worry about it. Not everyone has a great dad like yours. I'll be fine."

I nodded. I took my dad for granted. He was older than most of my friend's parents, and I often complained about his old-fashioned rules. Now I made a mental note to thank him when I got home for always being there when Mom and I needed him and taking time for his family despite his own long work hours.

After three hours of travel, the bus slowed and turned onto the exit marked for the college, then pulled into a parking lot with extra-long parking places for buses and vans. Standing up, Mr. Markenly gave us instructions. "You are welcome to break into whatever groups you choose so long as you adhere to proper conduct and remain within sight of me and the larger group. I will be mingling among the groups. Find me if you need anything. Oh, yes, and the art department has instructed that there are to be no pictures taken of art exhibits."

Reese, Draya, Sara, and I paraded across an open area where students who looked a few years older than us were gathered around a large fountain. Some were talking. Others had their phones in hand or were using tablets. A few looked up in interest as we went by.

Mr. Markenly led the way toward a building made of brick with large glass windows. The building was flanked by sculptures composed of different materials—wood, metal, even marble. There were a few structures that looked like someone had visited a junkyard then piled their findings in a heap to see how many objects they could stack without them toppling.

Our teacher opened a door into a large tiled room with white walls. A quick glance revealed exhibits arranged by artist. After a short welcoming speech from one of the college art professors, we started through the exhibits.

As we made our way from one display to the next, I was struck by the high quality of the photos. I could have spent all day studying the composition and light in each one. But Reese and Draya weren't as enthralled and moved more quickly than I'd like through the exhibits.

It was with regret I approached the last display. A man was standing in front of it, moving slowly from picture to picture. His brown hair was closely cut, and his blue eyes were intense as he studied the photos. He looked too old to be one of the college students Maybe a college professor? Or an artist?

I hung back right behind the man, willing him to move on so I could move closer to see the photos. As though sensing me there, the man suddenly turned and looked directly at me. His eyes widened as though startled to find me so close.

"Sorry," I muttered, stepping further back.

The man started to speak, but Mr. Markenly was approaching. He announced, "A few more minutes here. Then we'll hear from the director of the art department before walking to the cafeteria for lunch."

Draya had moved on down the room. Reese walked over to me. "Let's skip this last exhibit. The photos are all starting to look alike."

I shook my head. "I want to see it."

"Okay. Enjoy. I'm going to check out the soda machine I saw on the way in. I'll be back in a few minutes."

As Reese walked away, I turned to the last exhibit. The man I'd startled had moved off a few yards, so I had a clear view. I took in the overall effect with a glance, then stared in confusion. The air seemed sucked from the room as I took in what I was seeing. The eyes looking back at me were my own. But how could they be? There were no baby pictures of me. Yet here was a whole exhibit of portraits of me as an infant with my almost white hair, blue eyes, and unmistakable dimple.

I heard approaching footsteps and turned around, expecting to find Draya behind me. Instead, I found myself being studied by the man who moments earlier had been studying the portraits in front of me. Had he seen my surprise? Not just surprise, but shock even as I reacted to the photos?

The man was holding his phone up, and something in his gesture made me sure he'd just taken a photo. Of me? Or of the portraits? The portraits I knew were of me no matter however unlikely it seemed.

CHAPTER FIVE

Reese rejoined me. Placing his hand on my arm, he brought me back to my surroundings. "What's wrong?"

Looking up at him, I gestured toward the exhibit. "Those portraits! They are of me!"

Without meaning to, I'd raised my voice. The man who'd been studying the photos turned my way, his eyes studying me. He must be thinking I was a lunatic.

"Sorry," I mouthed his direction.

Reese took me by the arm and led me over to an empty corner. "What's going on?"

"Those photos in the last display are of me. The eyes. The hair. Even the blanket. They're too similar to the one on our wall at home for there to be any mistake."

Reese walked over to study the display for himself. The man had moved on to the far side of the display, but he still seemed to be staring my direction. Was his interest in the photo display or me? Was I mistaken that he'd taken a snapshot of me?

Well, turnabout was fair play. Pulling out my phone, I snapped a photo of the man through the openings in the display. I glanced at my phone. It was a clear photo considering how I'd taken it. I looked back up. That's when I realized the man was now approaching me.

I glanced quickly around for Reese and Draya. Reese was standing in front of one of the photos, head tilted, studying it.

Draya was nowhere to be seen. Then I was face to face with the stranger. Had he seen me take his picture? He had no reason to complain about it since I was fairly sure he'd snapped one of me.

"Summer?" The man's eyes studied my face as he went on tentatively, "I'd begun to think I'd never see you again. What are you doing here? Where is your mom?"

I backed away, the man's intensity making me uncomfortable, even a bit nervous. "I—you're mistaking me for someone else. My name isn't Summer."

"No I'm not mistaken. You're Summer, my daughter." He stepped toward me again, his blue eyes locked with mine. "You think I wouldn't recognize you? It's been years, but you still look like you did in those photos. The same eyes. The same dimple. Not to mention you look just like your mom when she was a teenager."

He turned to the exhibit, and for a moment his eyes were distant as he appeared to focus on the large portrait in the middle. Then he shook his head as though coming out of a trance and turned back to me. "Is that why you're here, Summer? Because of the photos? I knew your mom had to be here the moment I saw those pictures. But I'll admit I didn't expect to see you. "

My mouth was dry, and my mind couldn't formulate a coherent answer. I shook my head rapidly, hoping somehow things would start to make sense. "I don't know what you're talking about. Who are you?"

"You don't know who I am? Of course you don't! You were just a toddler when I saw you last. Hasn't your mother told you about me? Shown you any of the photos she took that day of me? Of me holding you? The three of us together?"

The man stepped forward and reached toward me. My heart raced. I needed to move, but my feet were frozen in place. Suddenly, Reese stepped between the man and me. "What's going on? What do you want with Bailey?"

The man's face registered confusion. "Bailey? Her name is Summer. It has to be. She looks just like her mom. That's her in those photos."

"You have her mixed up with someone else."

"I don't think so." The man looked directly at me. "Where is your mom? Where has she been hiding you from me all these years? She had no right."

Reese squared his stance. "You have the wrong person. Walk away."

"Not until Summer tells me where her mom is. She has something of mine. Something she stole from me."

Reese took a step toward the man, his jaw clenched. My heartbeat quickened. Was there going to be a confrontation between this stranger and Reese? I was relieved to see Mr. Markenly approaching with a fast stride.

"What's going on here?" he demanded.

The man hesitated, clearly wanting to say more. Instead he backed away from Reese and muttered, "Mistaken identity."

He swiveled on a heel and walked away. Mr. Markenly turned to me. "Anything wrong?"

I shook my head. "The man thought I was someone he knew."

"Okay, then. Probably just an honest mistake." Mr. Markenly's expression showed concern. "We have only a few more minutes. Then we'll hear from the director and head to lunch."

Draya came up, her eyes wide. "What's going on? I go to the restroom, and there's a confrontation?"

"Yes! It was creepy." I told Draya word for word as much as I could remember of what the man had said to me.

"So he thought you were here because the photos are of you?" Draya said.

I nodded. "And he thought my name was Summer."

"You also think the photos are of you," Reese pointed out.

"Look at them," I said. "The one in the center is almost identical to the one of me on the wall in our house. That's the same blanket with the same torn corner."

Reese studied the photos. "It does look like the same blanket. And I guess it could be you as a baby. But why would someone be displaying photos of you years after they would have been taken? And if they are of you, why would he be calling the person in the photos Summer?"

"Maybe it isn't such a mystery. Bailey, didn't you say you thought that portrait your parents have on the wall looked like it must have been done by a professional studio? Maybe it's as simple as the photographer finding Bailey's baby pictures in some old files and deciding they'd make a good art exhibit." Draya walked to the display and tapped the white card fastened to it. "Why don't we simply read the photographer's biography and find out?"

Of course! Why hadn't I thought of that? If Mom and Dad had done a photo package at some studio, that could explain the pictures. After all, some studios did insist on keeping the originals and even using them for marketing or other purposes if the contract didn't specify otherwise, however unethical that felt to me. But maybe that was because it was my baby face all over that display.

"Go ahead," I told Draya.

"Well, the title of the exhibit is 'Portraits of Summer.'" Draya put her hands on her hips. "Though these pictures look like they were taken in different seasons, not just summer."

"Maybe it means Summer as in a name," Reese interjected. "That man did say he thought Bailey's name was Summer."

"Keep reading," I urged. "What else does it say?"

"The photographer's name is Ashlyn Meadowbrook." Draya smiled. "What a pretty name for an artist."

"Obviously made up," Reese said.

"I like it," Draya protested. "Anyway, this Ashlyn grew up in the Chicago area, got a two-year degree from the Illinois Art Institute, and continued her education in New York City where she now lives."

My hope deflated. That was it? No information about the photos in the exhibit? There was certainly nothing in that short biography to tie this Ashley Meadowbrook to me. I hadn't been to Chicago before, and I didn't know anyone in New York City.

I slipped my phone from my pocket. We'd been instructed not to take photos of the exhibit, one reason I was pretty sure that man had been snapping a photo of me. But this was an emergency. I needed answers, and only by showing these photos to my parents would I get the right ones. I could always delete them later.

Being as inconspicuous as possible, I captured the exhibit on my phone. A few minutes later, the director of the art department, dressed in jeans and a polo shirt, entered the room. He spoke briefly, then handed out informational packs to those who were interested. I accepted one, then followed the others out the door and to the cafeteria.

Unlike our high school cafeteria, this one had different stations where students could make food selections. There was a bustle of activity as college students entered and found places at tables or took their trays and dishes to a dish pit before exiting. I would normally have been caught up in the energy, but worry filled me as we made our way to the tables reserved for our group. I continually glanced around for the stranger from the exhibit as I ate, not really tasting the food.

Reese looked across the table at me. "Bailey, I know you're upset about the man you encountered, and you need answers about the photos. Draya and I will help you figure out that mystery when we get home. But please don't let it take away from this experience and all the photography you've enjoyed today. You've looked forward to this trip all week."

I nodded. "The quality of the photography is amazing. Still, it's hard to get my mind off of what happened. What if you hadn't been there and the man had grabbed me?"

"You would have screamed loudly, and he would have taken off running like in the movies." Reese grinned, but I could see a hint of worry in his eyes.

CHAPTER SIX

It was close to four p.m. when we returned to the school. For me, the excitement of the trip had been dampened by the encounter with the stranger and long drive back to the school. Reese and Draya were quiet too as Reese drove Draya to her house and then me to mine.

Pulling up outside my house, Reese turned to me, concern knitting his eyebrows together. "Let me know what your parents say about the photos in the exhibit. Like Draya said, if those pictures really are you, I'm sure it's just this Ashlyn person using studio work from years back thinking no one would know the difference. And try not to worry about the man. Whoever he was, he's looking for the photographer who took the pictures, not you. Anyway, it's over, and he can't possibly know where you live, so hopefully you'll never see him again."

I wasn't so optimistic. After all, Reese hadn't heard the man claiming to be my father. But I nodded. "I'll talk to my parents about the photos when they get home. Until then I'll search online to see what I can find out about Ashlyn Meadowbrook."

Climbing out of the car, I waved as Reese drove off. Then I headed into the house, dropped my backpack on the floor, sat at the table, and studied the pictures of the exhibit I'd taken with my phone. I wasn't great at telling baby ages. But I could tell the subject, who I was still sure was me, looked to be only a few months old in the first photo and was a toddler chasing dandelion dust by the last one.

I flipped to the photo of the man who'd accosted me and

studied it. Who was he? And who was this person he'd mistaken me for? Were the pictures actually of someone named Summer who just happened to look so much like me I merely thought the photos were of me? As for the blanket with a torn edge in a field of daisies, was I overreaching to assume that proved the baby was me? Maybe this photographer had used that same blanket and settings for multiple photo shoots, of which I was just one.

I opened the laptop. Keying in the password, I sat staring at the screen. Since my parents had never liked me spending time online, I didn't possess research skills. Not sure what else to do, I tried a Goggle search. I typed in Ashlyn Meadowbrook, adding the word "photographer." Only one entry popped up, identifying the woman as creator of the "Summer" exhibit and giving the same short bio that had been posted at the exhibit.

I paused, trying to decide on the next step. What about photography magazines? Maybe Ashlyn Meadowbrook had written an article or published a photo. I found the website for *Creative Photography* and accessed an index of contributors. Yes! My heartbeat accelerated as the name Ashlyn Meadowbrook appeared highlighted in the search list. She'd won an award for the photo of the toddler chasing dandelion dust.

That was over three years ago. The only bio given with the photo was a single sentence saying the winner was a photographer from New York City. Why was there no press photo of Ashlyn with the announcement or one of her accepting her award? Sure, she was usually the one holding the camera. Still, shouldn't a professional photographer and award-winning artist have a basic press photo?

Maybe I could email the magazine and ask for the artist's contact information. I sighed. No, they likely wouldn't be allowed to give it to me without her permission. What I really needed was to talk to Mom and Dad. There was undoubtedly an easy answer to all of this. I simply couldn't think what it might be.

As if on cue, the sound of a car pulling in with a second car behind it was followed by doors shutting. My parents were arriving home together tonight. Even though both worked at the auto shop, Mom normally left earlier than Dad.

I quickly shut down the laptop, closing the lid as Mom stepped through the door followed by Dad.

"How was the trip?" Dad asked.

How did I bring up the pictures? Nothing came to mind.

Dad raised an eyebrow. "With all the talk about the trip this past week, I expected you to be bubbling over with enthusiasm."

The words spilled out of me. "It was good. But something strange happened."

"What do you mean?" Dad asked.

"There were pictures of me on display."

Dad's brows furrowed. "What are you talking about?"

"There was an entire exhibit of me. Baby pictures. At least I'm almost sure they were of me."

I expected Dad or Mom to say I was being silly. That the pictures couldn't possibly be of me. Instead, Dad looked at Mom, and for a moment, their eyes locked.

My heartbeat quickened as no one spoke because that silence said more than any words could have.

CHAPTER SEVEN

The silence lingered. Then Dad broke his gaze with Mom and turned to me. "You're saying you saw baby pictures of you at the exhibit?"

His face was filled with an emotion I couldn't identify. Confusion? Surprise? Even a bit of fear?

"Bailey." Mom broke into my thoughts. "Your dad asked you a question."

I pulled my phone from my back pocket. "We weren't supposed to take any pictures of the exhibits, but I needed you to see these photos."

I went to my gallery and opened the first picture. It was of the whole display. "The exhibit was called 'Summer' by Ashlyn Meadowbrook."

Taking the phone from me, Dad scrolled through the pictures with Mom looking over his shoulder.

"Well?" I demanded. "Is that me? As a baby?"

Dad cleared his throat. "They resemble photos we used to have of you. What did you say the photographer's name was?"

"Ashlyn Meadowbrook. Is that the name of the photographer who did that portrait of me on the wall? The one that looks like it was done in a studio?"

"No, that wasn't her name." Dad shook his head. "I'll look into this, okay? I'm sure there's an easy explanation."

"How?" I demanded. "I already tried Googling the photographer, and she's basically a ghost on the internet. And if she isn't the one who took that portrait of me, how did she get pictures of me? Or at least ones with the same blanket and background! Not to mention the same eyes and dimple and . . . and—"

Dad's brows furrowed as I broke off emotionally, but when he spoke, his voice was its usual calm tone. "I'll call the art department at the college and ask about the photographer. If that really is the same background, maybe this photographer bought the pictures off someone else. The person who did take your photos. I'm sure there's some easy explanation. You know what they say. Everyone has a twin somewhere. Maybe yours happens to have the same torn blanket."

As he spoke, Dad was scrolling again through the pictures. His eyes suddenly widened, and he held up the phone toward Mom. I leaned over to see what picture had brought on his reaction. It was the one of the man at the exhibit.

Dad turned to face me, holding out my phone. "Who is this?"

I wasn't about to mention the man's claim that I was his daughter, so I shrugged. "He seemed interested in the same exhibit. He spoke to me briefly, but he never mentioned his name."

"So why do you have his picture on your phone?"

I struggled for an explanation that wouldn't raise even more questions. "There was something about him. The way he was so interested in those same pictures. I took the photo on impulse."

Color rose in Dad's neck. "This is why I didn't want you to go on this trip. You have a photo of a stranger on your phone. How can I keep you safe from—?"

Dad clamped his mouth shut, his lips tight. Heat rose in me. My neck grew warm.

"Keep me safe from what? You were military. No doubt you can keep me safe from almost anything. And you've taught me a few moves to defend myself too. Why are you so upset? Do you know this man?"

Dad didn't answer immediately, then hunched his shoulders. "I thought he might be someone we used to know. But on second look, he doesn't seem as familiar as I'd believed."

I swallowed, my first impulse to hold back evaporating. "Well, maybe he really is. He certainly thought he knew me! He called me Summer, and he asked me something about my mom."

"What about me?" Mom asked in a rush. "Whoever this man is, he knows nothing about me."

"It was mistaken identity, obviously, since you are definitely not a photographer. He asked if I was there because of the photos. He said he was my dad and asked where my mom had been hiding me all these years."

Mom looked toward Dad, her face pale. No one spoke.

Then she looked at me for a few seconds before speaking. "That must have been scary. He clearly had you mixed up with someone else." Her voice held a slight tremble. "I hope you called security."

"No, Mr. Markenly came up just then, and the man left. But I think the man took a photo of me. That's partly why I took a photo of him . . . well, just in case he tried something creepy." I managed a grin at my dad. "Just being cautious like you taught me."

Dad cleared his throat. "Well, best to put this out of your mind. It was an unfortunate mistake."

He was saying all the right words, but something was off. I could feel it. Dad knew something about those portraits—and about the stranger. Something he didn't want to tell me.

In fact, neither of my parents' reactions weren't matching

their words. I needed to think. "Is it okay if I go to the park and take some photos? I want to try out the techniques I saw at the exhibit today." I was surprised at how normal I sounded.

"Sure. Go ahead dear," Mom said. She opened her mouth to say more, then closed it.

I grabbed my camera bag, the new compass catching my attention and alleviating my dark mood a bit. Leaving the house, I headed down our small street, then across several intersections until I came to a wooded park with trails. The sound of rushing water reached me before the rocky creek came into view. It was my favorite place to go when I needed to think.

Walking the path, I took some close-up nature photos and scenery shots. But I was too restless and worked up to concentrate, so after just a few minutes, I headed home. Entering the house, I heard raised voices from my parents' office. Instinct told me they were talking about the bombshell I'd brought home. Easing the door shut, I walked stealthily to a spot down out of view of the open office door but in clear ear shot.

Mom was talking. "What are we going to do about it?"

"I'm not sure it was him," Dad responded. "And he would have no way of knowing it was her."

Mom's sigh reached out into the hall. "You know it was him. He called her Summer."

"Well, how could we have known he'd be at the exhibit? It's been so long. I thought he was dead or in prison. And who is this Ashlyn Meadowbrook who has the pictures?" Dad's voice had a rare sharp edge.

"I don't know. Those are clearly April's. How would another artist have her photos?" Mom paused before adding, "Maybe nothing will come of it."

"I wish that were true. We need to be prepared. He knows she's in one of the high schools that visited the exhibit. Plus it seems probable he has a picture of her."

"At least he doesn't know her name," Mom said.

"He won't give up. Remember how he spoke to us before."

Dad didn't finish his sentence, and suddenly I heard his strong, firm footsteps crossing the office floor in my direction. If he stepped out, he'd discover his eavesdropping daughter. I silently fled back through the house and out the front door. I stood there a full minute before noisily reentering the house as though just arriving.

"I'm back," I called out, heading straight to my room so I wouldn't have to speak to my parents. I didn't think I could keep my confused emotions off my face, and I needed time to process what I'd overheard.

Funny, I'd always thought of my parents' lives as somewhat boring and routine. Now I wondered. They'd told me they thought they knew the man in the picture but had realized they must be mistaken. Yet from what I'd overheard, they not only knew the man's identity but were afraid of him finding me.

What secret were they hiding?

And how did I fit into it?

CHAPTER EIGHT

The next morning, Reese and Draya showed up at my door together. I waited until both Dad and Mom had left for work and we were settled around the table with French toast sticks and orange juice before telling my friends of the discrepancies between what my parents had told me and what I'd overheard.

Reese spoke first. "It sounds like there is a simple explanation. Someone took those pictures a long time ago. Your parents knew about it at the time but never expected to see the photographer in question again."

"Oh, I love a mystery!" Draya broke in, her face animated. Then she bit her bottom lip. "Sorry, Bailey. I know the situation is upsetting to you, but nothing ever happens here. We have to go clear to Chicago for excitement."

"It's okay. I need your help with this. How can we find out who the man is?" I asked. "My parents denied knowing him. I can't very well tell them I know they are lying. It sounds harsh even saying it aloud. And besides the man, there are two more people involved named Summer and April. From what I heard my mom saying, April was the one who took my original portrait photo and other pictures."

Draya's frown was thoughtful, but she quickly replaced it with a confident smile. "Let's start with what we do know. First, the photos in an exhibit in Chicago may be of you. Second, a stranger, also in Chicago, thought he knew you and called you

Summer. Third, the title of the exhibit was 'Portraits of Summer.'"

"Maybe that was a coincidence," I said. "Perhaps the artist meant the season. Some of the photos were taken in summer."

"One had snow in it," Reese countered.

"Okay. How about the artist? She has to tie into this somehow," Draya said.

"Can a photographer display pictures of a person without consent?" I asked. "Remember, our parents had to sign forms to have our photos on the school website, and mine didn't sign it. They said the internet isn't safe because you never know who will see your photos."

"Schools have different rules," Draya responded. "It's all about protecting 'minors" like us. A studio has full rights to any work it does unless there's a contract that says otherwise. I know because a friend of mine did a photo shoot for a modeling gig and was really upset when she saw some of her pictures in a sports catalog without even being asked or getting paid. The studio said she'd received the photos she'd paid for and any she didn't want belonged to the studio according to the fine print on her contract. After all these years, maybe this Ashlyn Meadowbrook never expected you or your parents to see her exhibit. Or else she herself had no idea who the child was if she got her hands on photos taken by someone else."

Draya pulled out her tablet. "Either way, just Googling a name isn't enough. We need to check whether this artist has any social media presence."

"You mean, FaceBook? Instagram?" I was probably the only teen on the planet without a FaceBook profile or any other social media presence thanks to my parents' paranoia about the internet.

"And YouTube. Pinterest. Twitter. Linked-in. Artists are like any business these days. They need a digital footprint if they are to gain traction." Draya's fingers flew over the keys, then she grinned. "Well, that was too easy. No social media profiles, but she does have an artist page."

"An artist page?" I asked.

"An online portfolio," Draya explained patiently. "Like a model might have, but these are of photos she took, not ones taken of her."

"Why didn't I find it when I searched for her name?" I said.

"Because your parents have all kinds of privacy settings on your laptop that get you into only the most public websites based on word recognition. Thanks to that computer camp I attended last year while you two were at adventure camp, I learned some topnotch research skills." Draya grinned. "Okay, and I also subscribe to a couple sites that hunt people down for you who don't have an online presence. You know, the kind that do a background check to see if your new boyfriend has a criminal record or find unlisted phone numbers and that sort of thing."

The kind my parents would have a fit if I signed up for. And I had a suspicion such sites required subscribers be adults. Not that such scruples would stop Draya once she was in research mode. Nor would the Pauls probably care from what I knew of their laid-back parenting. I felt a twinge of envy at the thought of a mom and dad who weren't constantly hovering over their daughter and worrying about her every move.

Leaning in over Draya's shoulder, I found myself looking at a page of photos that included all those I'd seen in the Summer exhibit and others as well. One that stood out was the word "Created" drawn in an elongated 3D graffiti style with shades of blue merging into purple. Stars appeared to be shooting out from it. The words "In Christ Jesus" were written in smaller letters underneath. The effect was amazing.

"Wow!" I exclaimed. "Did she draw that or merely take a picture of it?"

"I can't tell," Draya said. "Maybe both. It's part of an online exhibit of hers called 'Street Art.'"

"Created in Christ Jesus is a quote from the Bible. The book of Ephesians," Reese said. "The whole verse says, 'We are God's masterpiece. He has created us anew in Christ Jesus, so we can do the good things he planned for us long ago.'"

While his dad wasn't much on church, Reese and his mom had been attending the same church my family attended since shortly after their move, and in fact Reese paid more attention to what the preacher said than I usually did.

Draya arched her eyebrows. "And that all means what?"

Unlike Reese and me, Draya didn't attend church. Her mother had been raised Buddhist in Sri Lanka and her British father Anglican. Their compromise, Draya had told me years ago, was to ignore organized religion altogether, though they occasionally allowed her to attend youth activities with me. And Reese now that he was part of our trio of friendship.

"It means God gave us the talents to accomplish good things," Reese informed her now. "Not only for ourselves but for others and for God himself."

"That's a nice thought," Draya said.

Reese grinned. "And it's the truth. So your mad computer skills, my amazing soccer ability, and Bailey's awesome way with a camera are all from God. He gifted us with those things to use for good."

Draya swiped at her tablet screen. "Well, speaking of skills, let's look at the rest of these photos because I have to go soon."

"Me too," I spoke up. "I have to be at my parents' new shop at noon. Can you send the Created picture to my phone? It stands out to me."

Draya clicked some keys. "It won't let me send the photo. Probably some kind of use protection if this site is where the artist showcases work for sale. But I'll text you the link."

My phone pinged as the text came through. We spent a few more minutes browsing photos of me, other street art, and close-up photos of varied people. From young children to wrinkled seniors, every face was alive with emotion. Happiness. Grief. Fear. Anger. Bitterness. Compassion. It was all there in how the artist had captured their features.

"Wow. Ashlyn Meadowbrook is amazing," I said. "I'd love to meet her and learn how every picture she takes is so real."

"Well, if you're right and those photos are of you, then you've already met her," Draya pointed out. "The question is how and when."

"And how she ties in with that man at the exhibit who claimed my name is Summer and he's my father," I added.

"Not to mention the mother he claimed had hidden this Summer kid and stolen something from him," Reese commented.

I shook my head. "None of this adds up. My parents always told me I was their miracle child born when they'd given up having children. There's certainly no mysterious mother hiding me. And that man can't be my dad because I look like my actual dad. But there's that conversation I overheard. I mean, my parents are definitely hiding something."

"Whoa!" Draya held up a hand in stop sign mode. "That's a lot of questions. But there's an easy answer to most of them. The best way to confirm your parents are really your parents is to do a DNA test."

"Right!" I exclaimed. "I'll simply waltz into the auto shop and ask my parents for a DNA sample so I can take it to a lab. *After* I already brought up being adopted and they told me to my face that I wasn't. I can't wait for that discussion."

Draya laughed. "It's not like that anymore. You can do everything online now, including DNA tests. Let me look into it, and I'll let you know what we need to do."

"And the man's claim Summer's mom stole something from him? What do you think it could be? Money? Diamonds? Drugs?" Reese said.

I shrugged. "Your guess is as good as mine."

That ended our discussion. After dropping Draya off at home, Reese drove me to my Dad's new shop for my work shift.

CHAPTER NINE

Work helped take my mind off the questions I had. But on Sunday I broached the subject of the photo exhibit again. "Dad, did you ever find out anything about that artist?"

Dad frowned as he shook his head. "It's going to take time, Bailey. Remember, it's the weekend. The college is closed. I'll follow up Monday. Don't you think your mom and I want to know who has pictures of you on display as much as you do?"

"Draya found more photos posted by the same photographer online." The words were out before I knew I was going to say them. I bit my lip.

Dad fixed a penetrating gaze on me. "You went onto the internet to look for this photographer?"

I quickly sifted through possible answers. Ones that wouldn't get me into trouble. Finally I spoke. "I just typed her name into the browser. But nothing came up. That's as far as I could get on our laptop, as you know. And the laptops at school are even more search protected. But Draya has great computer skills, and she was able to track down the artist's webpage using her tablet. In addition to photos of me, Ashlyn Meadowbrook has photos of other people posted and street art too."

Mom's eyebrows went up. "Street art?"

"A fancy way of saying graffiti. Here, let me show you."

While I hadn't been able to access data on Ashlyn Meadowbrook, now that I had the link, my phone allowed me to open the webpage. I swiped until I found the Created photo.

"This is my favorite. Reese said it's from the Bible. From one of his favorite verses in Ephesians. You know, created in Christ Jesus to do good things and use the gifts and talents God gave you to help others and all that. At least that's what Reese says it means."

"So it is." Dad studied the photo, then seemed to relax. "And you certainly do have a gift for photography. I guess that's God's gift to you—and you are his gift to us."

Pulling me into a one-armed hug, Dad kissed the top of my head before quickly changing the subject. "It's beautiful out. How about I start the grill?"

I wanted to continue the discussion, but Dad was already out the door. He'd grill everything if Mom let him. Clearly the discussion was over as far as my parents were concerned. That left Reese, Draya, and me to continue searching for the answers I needed.

In the car Monday morning, Draya informed me she'd found a site for an online DNA test. "I ordered the kit. It will take a couple days to get here, then up to two weeks to process. One if we pay extra for a rush job."

Trust Draya not to wait for a go-ahead on *my* life and DNA before rushing in. I still wasn't even sure I wanted to take the test. Feebly, I responded, "Well, let me know how much it is so I can reimburse you."

Draya waved that off. "No worries. I put it on the credit card my parents got me for any unexpected expenses."

Translate that to Draya's parents being way richer than mine or Reese's and that they wouldn't even notice what charges she'd made on her discretionary spending card. Talk turned to summer plans.

"I wanted to go back to computer camp this summer," Draya said. "It really helped me with research skills. I'll be in Sri Lanka that week, so I'm out of luck. But you two are going back to adventure camp, right?"

"You bet!" I grinned. "I'm already signed up, and I can't wait. This year I'm even going to do the zipline. Last year I kept backing out."

I turned to Reese. "You'll zipline with me, right?"

His face hardened, his mouth tightening into a straight line before he responded curtly, "I'm not going to camp this summer. I'll be working full-time at my dad's company."

"But why?" I wailed. "We've been planning this for months! And you were hoping to go to soccer camp too. You saved the money for both camps so your parents wouldn't even have to pay."

Reese's fingers tightened on the steering wheel. "My dad says summer camp is for little kids. That it's time I stepped up and started taking responsibility in his business."

"But you're barely seventeen," I argued. "It's not like you're going to take over his company anytime soon."

"No, but he worked a full-time job every summer when he was a lot younger than me, and he says I'm way overdue to start. That growing up is about more than having fun." Reese frowned. "It's not that I mind having a job. I mean, I get his point, and I can certainly use the extra cash. The real problem is his expectations. He's made it clear I'm to start on the ground floor at his company summers and vacations so by the time I

42

finish college—a business degree, of course—I'll be ready to step in permanently to carry on the family business. He says camp and even summer soccer workouts are wasting my time and future."

"But you're an outstanding soccer player. That was going to get you a scholarship to college, so how is that a waste?" I protested.

"He doesn't see it that way. He said he can afford to pay my way, and no one with a brain is going to waste their life on something as chancy as sports. But he also made clear he'd only help with college if I took the major he chose—international business—and commit to working for his company."

Reese's shoulders were tense as he went on, "I love my parents. But I'm not a businessman like Dad. God made me an athlete. That's my gift. When I can't play soccer anymore, I want to be a coach or a physical therapist specializing in sports injuries. That's why I want to try for a sport's scholarship so I can pay my own way and choose my own future. But Dad did the whole 'you're a minor and under my roof, so what I say goes.' I doubt he's going to change his mind about this summer. But I'm not changing mine either about going for a sports scholarship even if I have to wait until I turn eighteen to apply and work my way through going to community college."

Reese stopped talking, and I knew from his expression that the discussion was over. Somehow the upcoming summer vacation didn't seem nearly as exciting knowing Reese and I wouldn't be sharing a week at camp this year.

During lunch, I went to the school library to see if there were any photography magazines, thinking maybe I could find something on the award Ashlyn Meadowbrook had won with my baby picture or anything else she'd published. But the few print magazines the school ordered were National Geographic and other educational titles.

Once home from school, I logged onto the internet and pulled up the website for Creative Photography where I'd found Ashlyn Meadowbrook listed as a contributor. This time I looked in the home page menu for a contact option. The link that popped up required inputting your own email address, then writing a short message in the text box provided. I wasn't sure what to say. Should I state boldly that this photographer's prizewinning photo was of me? That I was trying to contact her because I needed to know where she'd gotten my picture? The website moderator would likely think I was some crazy fan, stalker, or both.

In the end, I composed a simple message saying that I'd seen Ashlyn Meadowbrook's photo exhibit at a college and would like to get in touch with her to find out more about her work. That done, I felt compelled to get out of the house and away from the situation. There was nothing else I could think to do until Draya received the DNA testing kit, so I might as well pass the time with some picture-taking of my own.

As I retrieved my camera bag, I rubbed the back of my neck to ease a headache I felt coming on. How had my life gotten so crazy in such a short time? One day I was Bailey Collins, a normal almost-sixteen-year-old girl. Next day I had a stranger asserting he was my dad and claiming my name was Summer. If that wasn't bizarre enough, I'd overheard my own parents talking as though the man had been part of their past. My past too.

I rubbed the compass Reese had given me between my fingers and willed everything to go back to normal. But the ringing of my cell phone and Draya's number showing up on caller ID told me that wish wasn't going to be granted.

"Can you believe the DNA kit already arrived?" Draya bubbled enthusiastically. "There's basically just three small plastic bags with bar codes and a label you print names on and attach. You can swab cheeks with the long Q-tips they include. Or if the other parties involved aren't cooperating or don't know they are being tested, you can get ahold of a toothbrush they are using or hair from a comb or brush. So long as the hair strand has roots, as that's what gets tested. Then just put the three bags in the padded mailer they sent, and that's it."

"Wow, I thought it would be more complicated!" I exclaimed. "You're sure we don't have to have everyone's written consent?"

"Definitely not. Just think how the police do DNA profiles of suspected criminals. I rather doubt they ask the suspect's permission. Maybe this test wouldn't be admissible in court, but that's not why we're doing it. I get the feeling this site caters to a 'don't ask, don't tell' type of clientele."

I let out a silent sigh. Draya had clearly been watching too much Law and Order again. I broke in. "Fine, the toothbrushes should be easy. But I'll need to buy new ones first so I don't have to explain why everyone's toothbrush went missing at the same time. That might take a day or so until Reese has time after school to drive me to the drugstore."

"Oh, you don't need to do that," Draya interrupted airily.

"I've still got the card I used to buy the text kit, and I'm headed out shopping with my mom right now. I'll pick up some of those really nice battery-powered toothbrushes, and you can tell your parents our biology teacher recommended switching for hygiene reasons, so you bought one for each of you three. They'll throw out the old ones, and you can take them from the trash."

"No way!" I protested. "I can't let you do that on top of buying the test. Even if it is your parents' card. I appreciate everything you're doing. But my parents are paying me to work for them, so I have my own money."

"But I *want* to do this for you," Draya insisted. "Really! For one, I'm as curious as you are to solve this mystery. Who wants to wait a couple more days if it isn't necessary? If you're worried about cost, you can always pay me back when you're a rich and famous photographer. Anyway, I'll get the toothbrushes and have Mom drop me at your house on the way back."

CHAPTER TEN

An hour later, Draya was at the door, bag of battery-powered toothbrushes in hand. I took them from her. "Impressive! I've always wanted to try one of these, but Mom and Dad always figured it was a waste of money and batteries when good old hand-power can do the job."

"Well, since they're here and paid for, hopefully you can convince your parents to try them. Speaking of, your mom just pulled into the driveway."

The sound of a car door shutting reached my ears. Then the front door opened. I tried to look casual as I showed Mom the toothbrushes. "Mrs. White says these are far better at combatting bacteria and gum disease and preventing cavities than a regular hand toothbrush. I decided to give it a try and thought you might like one too.

Draya spoke up. "My family switched to these a couple years ago after our dentist recommended them. He insisted this particular brand is the one dentists prefer because research studies show them to be more effective."

She sounded like a television commercial. But Mom didn't seem to notice as she pulled a toothbrush from the bag. "Nice. Sure, we'll try them."

Mom turned to me. "I'm not sure if I mentioned that Dad and I will be going out Friday night. There's a play at the community theater Dad wants to see. It's been a while since we've had time for a date night, so we figured we'd go out to eat, then attend the play. Since we'll be out pretty late, I was thinking maybe you and Draya might enjoy one of your sleepovers. You haven't done that for a while either."

She glanced over at Draya. "If you don't have other plans, of course, and your parents don't mind. You could order in pizza, make popcorn, and have one of your movie marathons."

"That sounds fun," Draya said cheerfully.

I nodded agreement. But it wasn't thoughts of movie marathons, pizza, or popcorn that were suddenly churning in my brain.

"Well, I'd better get going now. I'll see you in morning, Bailey, and we can make plans for Friday." Draya's knowing glance as she headed out the front door told me our thoughts were moving on similar tracks.

The next morning as soon as Reese had picked us up, I gave Draya the used toothbrushes I'd collected. She had the padded mailer with printed label in her backpack. Dropping the toothbrushes in separate bags, she scribbled the names I gave her for each toothbrush on the bags, then sealed them in the mailer. Reese pulled over at a curbside mailbox, and Draya deposited the envelope through the slot. "They will email the results within two weeks. About the time school ends for the summer."

Reese glanced over at me. "What will you do if the results show your parents aren't really your parents?"

I shook my head hard. "I can't even go there. They've always been my parents. I've never questioned their miracle baby story. Besides, don't forget I look just like my dad. What would be the odds of that if I were adopted?"

I looked over at Draya. "I've been wondering if some of the answers might be in that lockbox. It's the only place in our house they could keep secrets they'd be sure I wouldn't see. Any ideas how I might get it open?"

Draya laughed. "I had a feeling that was your Friday night plan in addition to movies. But just because we taught ourselves to pick simple locks with paperclips from watching YouTube doesn't mean we could get an actual lockbox open. The lock is bound to be more sophisticated than anything I've done."

Reese was looking with astonishment from Draya to me and back. "Okay, I must have missed something here. Why in the world would you two be watching videos about lockpicking? Or learning to pick locks?"

Draya and I exchanged glances and grinned. I shrugged. "It was a really boring sleepover. We'd run out of movies and pizza. It seemed a good idea at the time."

"Well, I'll bring my tablet on Friday," Draya said. "Maybe we can find a YouTube tutorial on opening lockboxes. And I'll do some research in the meantime."

On Friday, Draya brought a duffel bag for her overnight stay and left it in Reese's car until he dropped both of us at my house after school. Mom was already home getting ready for their date night. Draya and I put on a movie, made popcorn, and chatted about casual school stuff while we waited for Dad to come home and my parents to leave for the evening. It seemed forever before both of my parents came downstairs.

Mom was throwing instructions over her shoulder even as Dad urged her toward the front door. "Don't be using the stove while we're gone. I'll never forget that little grease fire you two had making hamburgers. If you want to make something to eat, do it in the microwave. And you have our phone numbers if there's even the smallest problem. If there's a real emergency, call 911 first."

"Mom, we're not twelve anymore. And we got that fire out, remember? There was no reason to rush home then, and there sure won't be any reason now. Go enjoy yourselves."

Mom and Dad were finally out the door. Draya and I waited until their car started and we could no longer hear the engine before jumping to our feet. Draya grabbed her tablet and swiped it open before giving me a considering look. "You still sure you want to do this? Maybe this is all just some crazy misunderstanding."

"I hope it is," I answered. "The best solution here would be that the man was mistaken about knowing me, I was mistaken about those being my baby pictures, and my parents were mistaken in thinking they recognized the man in the photo. Because if there's been no mistake, then everything I thought true about myself isn't true. Including that my parents are actually my parents!"

"Well, thankfully the DNA test will tell us that," Draya said. "We should have the results by the end of next week. And if they do prove your parents are telling the truth, then the rest doesn't really matter. So maybe we should wait on that before trying to break into this lockbox."

I shook my head. "No. We might not get another chance with the house to ourselves. And my parents have been acting secretive all week. What about what I overheard? And Dad still hasn't done what he said he'd do about talking to the college art department and finding out where those pictures came from. No, even if the DNA tests show they are my parents and this man was mistaken, they are still hiding something. Like who is April? Why are they afraid of the man in the photo? How did Ashlyn get my pictures? And why does she have all those pictures of me as a baby and my parents don't?"

I headed down the hall toward the office, Draya trailing along with her tablet. "If I'm wrong and there's no big mystery, then I'll be glad to find that out. But it's obvious my parents are hiding something. And that lockbox is the one place I can think of that might hold the answers."

"Fine!" Following me into the office, Draya placed her tablet on the desk and dug out two paperclips from a pocket. "The good news is that I did find a YouTube tutorial that supposedly works on most lockboxes if they are at least ten years old. Any hope your parents' lockbox is as old as all the other furnishings in this house?"

"Probably. I can't remember the last time they bought anything new that wasn't clothes or household necessities."

Kneeling in front of the file cabinet, I yanked on the bottom drawer until it popped open. Lifting out the lockbox, I set it on the desk. Draya studied it closely. "Definitely at least ten years old. Maybe even twenty. This won't be much of a challenge."

Unbending a paperclip, Draya pulled it open and formed a hook on the end. Opening the other one, she left it straight with a bit of a curve. Then she went to work on the lock, explaining every step to me as she manipulated the paper clips. I rolled my eyes. This was my role in our friendship clear back to sixth grade. I listened while Draya figured things out and explained them to me as though I were her student.

Raising the lid on the lockbox, Draya straightened up with a triumphant smile. I was reluctantly impressed. "You really did that with two paperclips?"

I was just reaching past Draya for the lockbox when the sound of the front door opening and shutting floated down the hall. We looked at each other, the panic on Draya's face probably mirroring my own. I pushed the file drawer shut and snatched up the lockbox. Then we fled silently down the hall to my room.

"Oh, no! We left the office door open!" Draya raced back down the hall, eased the office door shut, and ran back to my room. As Draya closed the door behind us, I shoved the lockbox under my bed. Then we both flopped down on top of the bedcovers. A nervous giggle escaped my lips. Draya let out a second giggle. By the time Mom peeked into the room, we were lying side by side laughing hysterically.

"I'm glad to see you girls having fun," Mom said. "Wouldn't you know it? I left the play tickets in the office."

Draya and I listened in attentive silence as Mom's footsteps headed down the hall, then returned, heading toward the front door.

"Bye, Mom," I called out. "Hope the rest of your date is fun."

"Thanks, sweetie." We heard the sound of the front door closing behind Mom. Slipping down the hall to the living room, we watched until the car pulled out of the driveway and was once again out of sight. Then we returned to my bedroom, more alert to outside sounds this time. I knelt down and retrieved the lockbox from under my bed. Setting it on the bed, I raised the lid. A brown padded envelope was inside. I lifted it out. Underneath was a pile of photos.

"Photos?" Draya said. "Why lock photos in a safe box?"

I shuffled through the photos. "These are of my parents and grandparents. Mom told me there were only the few she gave me for the project. So that's already one lie we know for sure."

Turning my attention to the sealed envelope, I opened it as carefully as I could. Still, it was going to be obvious it had been tampered with. I tipped the contents into my lap. My eyes widened.

Draya's mouth gaped. "Are those photos of you?"

"I think so." I held up one of the photos. An infant swaddled in a blanket was cradled in a young woman's arms. Her hair was almost black though her eyes were light. "This is a newborn photo. But that's not my mom!"

"And that's a horrible hair dye job. Looks like she was trying for a Goth look." Draya studied the picture. "You don't have an older sister. Maybe a cousin?"

I shook my head. "Both of my parents were only children. And that's not a nurse or hospital worker because she's in almost every photo."

"This man is too." Draya held up a photo where the infant was balanced on the lap of a young man with blue eyes, shoulder-length brown hair, and a beard.

Taking the photo from her, I studied it. "Well, that's certainly not my dad. Could this be the man from the exhibit who thought I was his daughter? The one in the photo I overheard my parents talking about?"

I grabbed my phone and pulled up the photo I'd taken. Draya studied it, then looked back at the picture from the lockbox. "I guess the eyes could be the same. It's hard to tell. I mean, if this baby picture is you, it must be almost fifteen years old. Neither you nor that man look anything like this picture."

I shuffled through the remaining photos. "I don't understand. My parents have all these photos of me, yet they told me there weren't any."

"And they hid them," Draya added.

"This had to be at least part of what they were arguing about. But why all the secrecy?"

"I don't know," Draya said. "That's the big mystery here. I mean, I don't see anything in these photos that would make anyone want to hide them away for years and lie about them."

I sighed. "Me either."

"There is one thing, though, that's odd. It isn't merely that these strange people are in your baby pictures. It's that your parents aren't. I don't see a single picture here that has both you and them in it." Draya held up one of the newborn photos of me being held by the strange man and the woman. "Well, as they say, a picture is worth a thousand words."

I grimaced. "Or in this case, a picture is worth a thousand lies."

CHAPTER ELEVEN

Draya and I talked long into the night. I woke to my mom opening my bedroom door. It seemed like I'd just closed my eyes, but a late spring dawn was slanting through the windows.

"Bailey, wake up." Mom's voice was soft but stern.

I sat up groggily. Mom held up a tablet. "I found this in the office. I'm assuming it's your friend's as it sure isn't yours. Why don't you explain why it was on the floor in front of the file cabinet—and why either of you were in the office in the first place."

I swallowed hard. How had we forgotten Draya's tablet? She'd set it down when we opened the drawer, and we'd never picked it up. Mom hadn't yet mentioned the missing lockbox.

"Bailey, I'm waiting."

"I'm thinking," I said, finding it hard to focus on such little sleep. Stretched out on the carpet in a sleeping bag, Draya didn't even stir.

"Try the truth. That's the easiest story to tell."

"You won't like the truth."

Mom's face paled. "Tell me."

I dragged myself out of bed, still groggy despite the seriousness of the situation. Grabbing a clean outfit, I shook my head hard, trying to come fully awake. "Let me shower and wake up first, okay?"

Mom nodded. "We'll let your friend sleep, but if she was in

there with or without you, I need to know."

Twenty minutes later, I was sitting across the table from my mom, orange juice in hand. She looked into my eyes. "Tell me what's going on."

I took a sip of juice, stalling, trying to figure out what to say. Should I tell her I have the photos? She must already know. Draya's tablet being in front of the file cabinet would be a big giveaway. I looked up and met her gaze. "I have serious questions, and I think you have the answers I need."

Mom met my gaze for a few seconds, and neither of us looked away. Then she spoke. "I know you have the lockbox. Did you get it open?"

"Yes. Draya picked the lock. It was wrong, but I knew you were hiding something from me. Who are the man and woman in the photos, and why did you hide the pictures?"

"There's no easy answer. I knew the photos would raise questions we might not be able to answer."

"Why? What difference does it make if someone else is holding me in those photos? I simply want to know who it is."

"It's your dad's much younger half-sister and her boyfriend. Since we'd never told you about her, it didn't make sense to bring it all up over a few photos for a school project."

"I didn't think we had any relatives."

"Dad's father, your grandfather, lost his first wife to cancer when your dad was in his teens. When your grandfather was in his early forties and Dad had just graduated from high school and enlisted in the Navy, your grandfather married a woman twenty years younger than himself. He and his new wife had a baby a year after they were married. Her name was April."

Mom paused.

"Go on," I urged.

"Dad only saw his new half-sister occasionally when he went home on leave from the Navy," Mom continued. "And your grandfather's second marriage didn't last. When April was five, your grandfather and her mother divorced. After that, April lived with her mom. By then your dad and I were married. But we moved around so much with the Navy we didn't see much of her. Dad tried to arrange visits with his half-sister when he wasn't at sea, but April's mom wasn't interested."

"So why all the secrecy?"

Mom sighed deeply. "It was a difficult time with difficult memories. When April was in high school, her mother overdosed on drugs. April came to live with us. We were happy to have her, especially since we had no children of our own then. But she was a hard teen to parent. With her addiction issues, April's mother had never really been there for April, much less parented her. April had pretty well raised herself and wasn't used to having house rules. So when we made clear there was a certain behavior code we expected in our home, she rebelled. She took off as soon as she turned eighteen."

"But she's in those pictures," I pointed out. "So she must have come back to visit."

"She did, but things didn't really get better, and she didn't stay for long. Like her mother, April and a boyfriend she'd met at art school were deep into the drug scene. And by then we had you. Neither of them were healthy people to have around a child. And then they were both gone, and we haven't seen them since. We only kept the pictures because they're all we have of you at that age. But it's too hard to look at them without remembering the heartbreak. So we put them away. I hope you can understand why we preferred not to bring them up or that time period. After all, you don't even know them."

Mom stood, and the discussion was over. Yet the need for more answers haunted me. For one, how had these baby pictures taken with a half-aunt and her boyfriend survived while all those with my parents in them had been mysteriously misplaced? Had that missing thumb drive ever even existed?

CHAPTER TWELVE

Steps sounded outside. The door opened, and Dad came in. "You haven't left for the shop?" Mom asked.

"I was fixing a problem I had with the mower last time I cut the grass," Dad said. "Now I can mow as soon as I get home from work."

"I explained to Bailey about April. She found the photos we had put away." Mom and Dad exchanged a meaningful look, but neither said more.

I finally asked the question burning my brain. "So if my baby photos were on a thumb drive that went missing, and you never got around to printing any, why are there prints with this April and her boyfriend but not with you?"

Mom gave Dad another quick glance. He spoke up. "April took those and later gave them to us. Otherwise we'd have none of you from that age at all."

There was no mistaking the truth in his voice, and it was a reasonable answer, so I dropped the subject. "Do you know where she is now? Your sister?"

Dad shook his head, a sad look coming across his face. "She disappeared back into the drug scene when you weren't more than a toddler. We tried for years to find her but never could. We finally concluded she must have died of an overdose or she'd have popped up somewhere. There's a lot of Jane Does who aren't identified because they're on the streets when they die and have no I.D."

"In any case," Mom broke in, "It's just as well you know now that you're old enough to understand the situation—and why this is painful for your dad especially. She was his baby sister, and the uncertainty of not knowing what happened to her has been difficult. So I hope you understand why we put those photos away and have preferred not to revisit those difficult memories."

"But the photos are of me too," I argued. "And April was my aunt. I get why you wouldn't have told me when I was little. But is there any reason we shouldn't keep those pictures out now?"

Dad shot a glance at Mom, who gave an almost unperceivable shrug of one shoulder. What was that about?

"I don't have time to talk about this right now," Dad said. "I need to get to the shop. But if it's okay with your mom, I see no reason to put the photos away again now that you've seen them. How you got them is a different issue. Whatever your reasons, breaking into our office and a box clearly locked for a reason isn't okay. We'll deal with that when I get home from work."

Movement caught my eye. Draya was standing out of my parents' sight. How much had she heard? Feigning innocence, she entered the kitchen with a cheery good morning.

"Good morning, Draya, dear," Mom said. "Did you sleep well?"

Draya yawned and nodded.

"I have to get to the shop too," Mom said. "This is a really busy weekend for our new shop site. I wish I had time to make you breakfast, but you're on your own."

"Do you mind if we invite Reese over for breakfast too?" I

asked. "I was thinking of making pancakes and bacon for Draya. Then we were going to do some studying for finals. I know Reese has to study for finals too."

Draya chimed in, "We'll make sure the kitchen gets cleaned up too so you don't have to think of a thing but your new shop."

"I'm taking you at your word you'll be studying. No more snooping around," Mom said.

By the time Dad and Mom were out of the driveway, Draya was already on her phone calling Reese. I went to the refrigerator to pull out bacon, eggs, and milk, then got the pancake mix from the cupboard. I was anxious to hear what Reese thought about the pictures we'd found and Mom's explanation.

Because I for one was sure we still didn't have the whole story.

CHAPTER THIRTEEN

Reese arrived as Draya was draining cooked bacon on a paper towel. He snatched a piece, and she swatted his hand with a pancake turner.

He yanked his hand back. "Ouch. That smarts."

"Don't touch the bacon until the pancakes are ready," she said, wielding the spatula.

Reese snatched another piece of bacon but jumped back before Draya could smack him again. "So what's going on?"

Draya dropped the last of the pancakes on a plate and set them on the table. "The lockbox was full of photos."

We filled him in while we ate. Draya and I finished quickly, then waited impatiently for Reese to clean up at least half the bacon and the final three pancakes. Draya cleared the dishes from the table while I got the envelope and poured the contents onto the table.

Reese glanced at the pile of photos, looking at a few more closely. "So the woman is your aunt, and the man is her boyfriend? And you never knew you had an aunt?"

I shook my head, then nodded since his questions called for both. "Mom said the man was April's boyfriend. But I couldn't very well ask if he was the same man who spoke to me at the exhibit since they don't know I eavesdropped on that conversation."

"That's right. I forgot." Reese picked up a photo in which

baby me was being held by the boyfriend. "You think it's the same guy? I don't see it."

Draya picked up the photo and turned to me. "Bailey, let me have your phone for a moment."

I handed it to her and watched as she sent the photo of the man from the exhibit from my phone to hers. Then she emailed it to her computer account. She used her phone to photograph the picture of the man holding me and sent it to her computer also.

"What are you doing?" I asked.

"We might be able to find out if it's the same man," Draya said, opening a photo editing program on her computer. She put the uploaded photo of the man at the exhibit next to the photo of the man holding me as an infant. Isolating the face in each picture, she cropped out the rest of the photos so the two faces were side by side.

"They look nothing alike," I said. The surge of disappointment filling me made me realize how much I'd been hoping they were the same person. That would have been another clue to the mystery of how my photos ended up at the exhibit.

"Be patient." Draya used an erase tool to remove the hair and beard from the old picture and the hair from the new picture.

My mouth gaped as I stared at the results. There was no question. The two men were the same, the only difference being obvious signs of aging.

"Incredible," Reese said.

Draya smiled. "Right?"

"What does this mean?" I asked.

"It means the man watching you at the exhibit was at one time your aunt's boyfriend," Draya said. "A bigger question is how he ended up there coincidentally right when you walked in."

"Well, you said he was looking for the person who took the photos," Reese pointed out. "Maybe he knew the photos were going to be there and hoped the photographer would be there as well. Being there at the same time as Bailey had to be a coincidence since we didn't even know ourselves until a week ahead."

"Well, now I wish I'd talked to him," I said. "He might have information that could help explain some of the mystery of my background."

"Maybe," Reese said. "But I'm not sure it would have been safe to talk to him. I mean, you heard your dad. If this man in the photos is the same guy, then we know he was into the drug scene. And it didn't sound like he wanted some family reunion. He claimed to be your father, and he said he was looking for the photographer because he wanted something she'd stolen from him. For all we know, if you'd stuck around he might have tried to abduct you."

"Really?" I stared at Reese. "This isn't a crime drama. It's my life. And however crazy and complicated it's getting, kidnapping seems a bit far-fetched."

"I don't know why," Reese argued. "After all, your aunt disappeared, and your dad said she and this guy were both into drugs. And drugs mean crime just like in all the crime shows."

Draya and I rolled eyes at each other before she spoke up firmly. "Let's get back to the business at hand. Did your parents give you a name for this boyfriend? Or your aunt?"

"My aunt's name was April. If her mom was married to my dad's father, her last name should be Collins like ours. Unless she got married since my parents saw her last."

"So let's try a search for April Collins." Draya tapped on some keys, and pictures began filling her screen. There turned out to be hundreds of April Collins on the internet. But none looked like an older version of the woman holding me in the baby photos.

"Don't be disappointed," Draya said. "Her hair was obviously dyed in the photos we saw. And it was short. She could have let it grow out and back to its original color."

"True. I don't think I'd recognize her in that case," I admitted.

Draya finally gave a sigh and shut down her computer. "I need to take a break. I don't think I can stand to look at one more April Collins."

"We all need a break," I agreed. "Remember how we'd have sleepovers, Draya, and get up before my parents for Saturday morning cartoons? I'm in the mood for being twelve again."

"Your mom said we're supposed to be studying," Draya pointed out.

Reese grinned. "We studied computer research skills. That should count for something."

Nodding agreement, we dropped onto the couch side-by-side and surfed channels until we found a show we all agreed on.

CHAPTER FOURTEEN

The next week was busy with completing final class projects and studying for exams. The only time Reese, Draya, and I had to talk was the drive to school and back. Draya was still poking around the internet for any mention of Dad's half-sister April or the photographer Ashlyn. But she was too focused on maintaining her perfect grade point average to give it much attention, and I was too busy trying to finish the year on the honor roll to push.

I hardly saw Mom and Dad either as they were working long hours getting the new shop set up and dealing with an increase in business that had them both in a good mood. Having breakfast and supper together as a family had always been part of our family routine no matter how busy we all got. But this week breakfast had been a fast bowl of cold cereal before dashing out the door, and Mom had called three separate evenings to let me know I should grab a frozen dinner as they were running late at the new shop.

"I'm so sorry about this," she'd apologized hurriedly. "I feel like we're neglecting you horribly. But I promise this won't continue. We're almost done the unpacking, so next week should be back to regular shop hours."

I assured her I wasn't feeling neglected. But I had to wonder if my own parents weren't trying to avoid me so they didn't have to answer any more awkward questions. On Wednesday, one of the evenings they'd run late, Dad poked his head into my bedroom as I was heading to bed.

"Hey, just wanted to let you know I finally heard back from that college you visited. I'd left a voice message with the art department twice asking for information on that photography exhibit. I'm sorry to say the only information they gave me was what you already had. The artist was Ashlyn Meadowbrook, and they weren't authorized to give out any personal information on her."

I nodded as there was nothing more to say at this point. At least until the DNA results arrived, I was at a dead-end, and I wasn't about to let my GPA drop below an A-minus for a mystery I had no reason to believe wasn't exactly what my parents had told me. Or a real mystery at all. Until final exams were over, I decided to just assume the strange man at the exhibit had mixed me up with someone else, Ashley Meadowbrook had been the photographer of my baby pictures, and Summer was some other baby she'd photographed using the same torn blanket.

Except the pictures we'd found and the conversation I'd overhead contradicted everything else.

Finally, the last day of school arrived. This was only a half-day. I felt good about how my exams had gone. Draya, of course, was in no doubt she'd aced hers. Reece had stayed behind for some team meeting with the soccer coach about summer practice, so for once Draya and I had to take the bus home. I was still hoping for Reece's sake that his dad would at least let him practice with the team during the summer.

"Hey, you want to get off at my house?" I asked Draya as the bus neared my stop. "We haven't hung out in a week, and you're leaving for Sri Lanka in eight days. I'm working at the shop this coming week before I leave for adventure camp, so we might not get another chance before you go."

"Sure, let me check with my mom." Draya dragged her cell phone from a pocket. "This is actually good timing since your parents won't be home for a few hours. Now that exams are over, I've been wanting to get back to the mystery of your baby pictures. Any chance of taking another look at what we found in the lockbox? We got interrupted last time. Maybe we'll find something we missed."

I had to laugh. Trust Draya to turn a final girl-time into a research session. I hadn't decided if she was going to turn out a computer scientist like her mom or win Pulitzer prizes for investigative journalism.

Draya sent a text and seconds later received one in return. "Mom says sure. Dad will pick me up at your house on the way home from his office."

A bus stop and after-school snack later, Draya and I sat on my bed, the photos Mom had let me keep from the lockbox spread out around us. But no matter how long and hard we looked at my baby pictures, they didn't reveal any information about April or her boyfriend, whom we were assuming to be the strange man at the exhibit.

Dropping a particularly adorable picture of me showing off my first tooth, Draya reached over and picked up a stack of photos we'd set aside since I wasn't in them. Shuffling through the stack, she stopped and held up the photo of Dad in uniform saluting an older officer. "Isn't this your dad?"

I nodded.

"You're sure?"

"Of course I'm sure. Even turned sideways, he looks exactly like he does now minus twenty pounds and some gray hair."

Draya held the picture out to me. "Look at the name tag on the uniform shirt."

I did what she said, but with my dad turned away from the camera, I couldn't make out all the letters. Still, one thing was clear. The last name on the uniform was most definitely not Collins. "What does it say? I can't read all the letters."

Draya pulled out her phone and took a snapshot of the photo. Then she enlarged the name tag. It was now easy to read the last name, *Hill*.

I rubbed the back of my neck where a headache was starting to form. "What does this mean? Dad's last name isn't Hill! Maybe he's wearing someone else's uniform."

"You mean, like he ran out of clean laundry and borrowed another soldier's shirt?" Draya looked skeptical. "And for something as important as whatever this ceremony was? I'm no expert on the military, but does that even sound like your dad?"

"No," I admitted.

As organized, methodical, and downright control-freak as my dad had always been, I couldn't even picture him running out of clean clothes or showing up in public less than pressed and polished. He treated his auto shop as though the flight deck of a Navy carrier and carried respect for our nation's military to such an extreme I counted myself lucky I didn't have to salute for the weekly bedroom inspection he'd carried out well into my early teens. Wear another man's uniform while saluting what was clearly a high-ranking officer? I didn't think so!

"But that's definitely not his name," Draya pointed out reasonably. "So either he's wearing someone else's uniform, that isn't your dad, or he's changed his name. Take your pick."

I let out a loud sigh. "This gets more and more crazy. I'm sure there's some logical explanation."

"Like there is for that man calling you Summer and saying you're his daughter?" Draya's eyes lit up. "Hey, maybe your parents are in the witness protection program! That would explain all of this. These pictures are all part of the life they had to leave behind. That's why they're hidden."

I groaned. "Sure, and I'm a character in some Tom Clancy movie and my dad's James Bond!"

I broke off, suddenly thoughtful. Farfetched or not, maybe Draya wasn't so crazy. It would certainly explain that man calling me by a wrong name. Jumping off my bed, I walked down the hall. Draya followed at my heels as I entered the living room, looking around with new eyes. Why had I never noticed before?

"What?" Draya demanded, bumping into me from behind when I made an abrupt stop. "I can hear the wheels turning in your brain!"

"The walls. The office. Our whole house. Anyone could live here. There's nothing to show who we are. Nothing personal."

"There's that photo of you," Draya pointed out.

"One photo in the whole house. I've seen your house. Everything in it says something about you. Even about your mom's family in Sri Lanka and your dad's family in England. But us? No photos, no relatives—except this new aunt I never knew about. No old family friends. No vacations. My parents don't seem to have any out-of-town friends, only the people at church. You'd think my dad would stay in touch with guys he served with in the Navy at least. Unless—"

"Unless they were in the witness protection program." Draya repeated, her eyes intense. "Hey, let's do a search using the name on that uniform. We'll look for a Timothy and Patty Collins first. If they pop up, we'll know we were wrong. If they don't, we'll try Timothy and Patty Hill. And your aunt too. We didn't find anything on April Collins. But if your dad's last name was originally Hill, his sister's name would be April Hill."

I shook my head. "If this is for real, don't you think they'd have changed first names too?"

Draya frowned. "Maybe. But in the movies they often keep the first name when they get a new identity. You know, because it's a whole lot harder to react to a new first name than remembering a last name. Anyway, we can at least try."

I didn't argue since Draya's parents let her watch a lot more movies than mine did. Though I wasn't too sure Hollywood could be depended on to get the finer details of law enforcement or spy craft right. I looked over her shoulder as Draya typed the name Timothy Collins on her tablet.

"A lot of people don't have a web presence," she commented. "But I subscribe to a people search engine that gets you into all kinds of databases that aren't public. Not anything illegal or anything, but court files that show if they have a criminal record or government records that show if someone has incorporated a business or bought property or even has a driver's license or state I.D."

Of course Draya would subscribe to such a service! Definitely a Pulitzer Prize in her future. Her fingers raced across her tablet keyboard. My heart raced as page after page of hits came up. Finally some answers. But my excitement soon deflated when I realized none of these Timothy Collins were the right one. I reached in and clicked on the images link to see if Dad's picture might show up. But not one image was of my dad.

Draya repeated the process with the name Patty Collins, Timothy and Patty Collins, then Timothy and Patricia Collins. Again nothing, not even a driver's license, although a picture did pop up of Collins Auto Repair.

"It's like my parents don't exist," I said with despair. "Not just in the past, but now!"

"Well, they obviously do exist," Draya said reasonably. "You'd think they'd at least have a driver's license. I mean, isn't that what they do in witness protection—give you a new identity that shows up in the system? Maybe that's why your parents are so sticky about driving under the speed limit and all that. They're worried they might get pulled over and have to show a license. Here, let's try Timothy Hill."

Again there were pages of results, and my eyes scanned them for any sign of my dad. Again we came up empty handed.

"Maybe he's gone by the new name so long there's nothing on the internet from his old life," Draya suggested. "You told me once your dad left the Navy before you were old enough to remember. If he was using the name Hill in the military, those records would still be there. Unfortunately, a $99.99 annual subscription isn't going to get me into that level of government records."

"At least now we know why my parents are so uptight about social media and the internet," I said despondently. "But is it to keep me from finding out there is no Tim and Patty Collins or to keep someone else from finding that there is? They sounded really spooked about this boyfriend running into me in Chicago."

"Chicago," Draya repeated thoughtfully. "My friend Devon who graduated last year went to boot camp at a Navy base there. I think there's more than one base in fact."

"That's right!" I responded, suddenly excited. "Including one of the biggest Navy bases in the country on the Great Lakes. I wonder if that's where Dad was based when that picture was taken. Or when his sister was living with them. Maybe whatever happened to make Mom and Dad change their name was in Chicago, and that's why Dad has been so paranoid about me going there even for a field trip."

"Maybe," Draya agreed. "It makes as much sense as anything else. Let's see if we can find anything on an April Hill who's ever lived in Chicago."

But though countless April Hills in Chicago and elsewhere popped up, none indicated any connection to my parents. Draya and I spent another hour trying out all kinds of name combinations. The arrival of her father to pick her up forced us to give up for the time being.

"Maybe we'll find something out when the DNA results come," Draya consoled me. "I'm expecting those any day now."

I was watching a movie when my parents arrived home. They sounded cheerful as they entered the house, still discussing their day's work at the auto shop.

"Hi, Bailey," Mom called out. "Did you have a good last day of school? I've already ordered pizza to celebrate. Should be here in ten."

"It was okay. Draya came over for the afternoon. She just left." I couldn't stand it any longer. Drawing in a deep breath, I blurted out, "Are you guys in the witness protection program?"

Dad's mouth dropped open. Mom let out an audible gasp and looked at Dad.

"It's okay," I said quickly. "Draya and I were looking at those old pictures and saw that the name tag on your uniform said Hill instead of Collins. We did some research. When we couldn't find any actual Tim or Patty Collins, we kind of figured it out. I know now that's why you've always been so overprotective of me."

"I—" Mom stammered, looking again at Dad.

Dad took a step forward, his expression suddenly stern. "Bailey, this is too much. First breaking into our lockbox, then using your friend's computer skills to do a background check on us? I would never have expected such behavior of you."

"But—" I interrupted. "I didn't mean to . . . I just wanted to understand . . . I mean, you never talk about . . ."

I broke off, fighting tears. Mom stepped forward and put her arms around me. "It's okay, honey. I can understand why you'd be curious about your aunt and our past. Just because it's painful for us doesn't mean you wouldn't want to know more as you got older. We should have realized."

Dad's hand came down on my shoulder. He said heavily, "I'm sorry I snapped at you, honey. That wasn't right. Please believe me that we are *not* in some witness protection program.

That said, sometimes adults have good reason to put their past behind them and to keep certain matters private. It was precisely to avoid this kind of misunderstandings that we'd locked the pictures away. Maybe one day when you're older, we can share more. For now, I am going to have to ask you to drop this subject and trust that your mom and I have good reasons for what we do."

"And I know Draya is your best friend," Mom added, her tone exasperated. "But we'd appreciate if you'd stop sharing private family matters with her. Or Reese. Understood?"

I swallowed. "Understood."

"I need the pictures back. I'm going to remove temptation by putting them away."

Silently, I went to my room, retrieved the stack of photos, then returned to the living room and handed them to my mom. I held my breath, hoping it wouldn't occur to either of my parents that I had copies of some of those photos on my phone. As un-techie as they both were, neither brought it up.

"I'm sorry about this," Dad repeated, giving me a hug. "I love you, honey. And I hope you will always trust your mom and me to do the right thing for this family. Now I'm trusting you to let this subject drop. I'm making my own inquiries as to this photographer who has your pictures. If something turns up your mom and I feel you should know, you'll be the first to hear."

The doorbell rang just then. Dad answered the door and came back a few moments later with a pizza box. We all dug in, chatting about my last day of school and the new shop as though the previous horrible conversation had never happened. I barely choked down one slice before making an excuse that I was tired and heading for bed.

I could hear my parents' voices turn serious and drop to a murmur the moment I was out of the room. Were they talking about my transgressions? And what was so bad in their past they couldn't talk about it? Surely a relative with drug problems wasn't so unusual they needed to hide it.

And if they weren't in some witness protection program, why did my parents appear to be virtual ghosts? Exactly who were Tim and Patty Collins?

Or Bailey Collins, for that matter?

CHAPTER FIFTEEN

Our house was silent the rest of the weekend. On Saturday, my parents were both booked solid at the repair shop. On Sunday morning, rushing through breakfast and off to church kept us from having to really speak. After church, we went out to a Chinese buffet with a couple other church families. We were just walking into the house when my cell phone rang. It was Draya.

"I got an email from the DNA lab," she said excitedly. "I haven't peeked. I'm coming over."

"No, that isn't a good idea," I said. "Let me see if I can come over to your house."

I was torn whether to tell Draya about my conversation with my parents. At minimum, I needed to let her know I'd been ordered to drop our investigation.

My parents had both paused to watch me take my call. I pasted a smile on my face. "That's Draya. She's all excited about her trip to Sri Lanka and wants to get together with me. And Reese too."

I figured that wasn't stretching the truth since Draya was excited, did want to see me, and would want Reese to be there if possible for the big reveal. "If Reese can pick me up, do you mind if I pop over for a couple hours?"

Dad and Mom gave each other that parental glance. Then Dad said, "I see no reason why not. Just keep in mind what we discussed the other day."

"Oh, I'll keep it in mind, alright!" I answered heatedly, then broke off. Dad was fairly easy-going, but he was hardnosed about being respectful to grownups and all that. More of that military training, I guess. If he decided my tone was even a bit disrespectful, I could forget about calling Reese for that ride.

"I got it, Dad," I said more calmly. "In fact, this will be a perfect opportunity to let them know I've talked it over with you and I've got all the answers I need."

And that was a lie! Heading to my room, I called Reese. I'd seen him and his mom at church, though we'd only exchanged a few words, so I didn't expect any problem with asking him for a ride. But when I got him on the phone, he sounded irritated.

"I can't talk now. I'm with my dad at his office. He's been showing me what I'll be doing this summer."

"On a Sunday?" I said incredulously. "I mean, you're starting work for him tomorrow, right? I'd think he'd at least give you the weekend to recover from exams if you're going to be working all summer."

Reese let out an audible breath. "Sure you'd think—if you didn't know my dad. He says he can't afford to waste billable hours getting me lined out, especially since he's leaving on his trip in the morning and he expects me to report for duty to his manager at eight a.m. It's not like I chose this. I'd rather be with you."

"I understand. I'm just disappointed. I leave for camp tomorrow, and Draya leaves Wednesday, so this is the last chance for all of us to hang before Draya gets back from Sri Lanka. We had some new leads on those photos we were going to check out. But no big deal. Draya and I can do that. And I'll see you maybe next weekend when I get back from camp."

I bit off my words. Reminding him I'd be going to camp without him probably wasn't the best conversation choice. I wanted to tell him about the new mystery of Dad's uniform having a different name and that Draya had received the DNA results. But I knew that would make Reese feel even worse about not being able to join us. Whatever new info we found could wait until he was free.

"I'll plan on that," Reese said. "Tell Draya to have a safe flight for me. And text me if anything exciting turns up on your new leads. I'll try to find a chance to call you before you leave for camp. Otherwise when you get back. I'll probably still be at work, but at least shoot me a text when you leave camp."

The adventure camp required campers to turn in their phones on arrival. Something about making teenagers take a break from their tech and concentrate on nature and developing relationships instead of looking at their screens all day.

"I'll do that."

Once Reese rang off, I called Draya back. "Reese can't give me a ride. Any way you can make it over here?"

"Sure. I'll take an Uber. My parents just got me the app and set it up with a credit card so they don't have to drive me everywhere."

Of course they had! My parents would tell me to walk if it was important enough. A half-hour later, I let Draya in the front door, her computer bag over her shoulder. My parents had retired to their bedroom for the Sunday afternoon nap that was one of their rituals if they didn't have to be anywhere else, so I didn't have to explain my change of plans.

The moment we reached my room, Draya dug out her laptop and opened it. Logging in, she brought up her email, then clicked on the one with the DNA results. Another click opened an attachment. "I listed your family as mom, dad, and daughter."

I leaned over, trying to make sense of the graphs and percentages on the PDF that now showed on the screen. In truth, I was less interested in the DNA report than digging further into the mystery of Dad's uniform and last name. Whether or not Timothy and Patty Collins were my parents' real names, it had never seriously crossed my mind that they weren't my real parents. So Draya's unbelieving gasp made me jump.

"Oh no! That can't be right." Draya pointed at a results bar.

I leaned in for a closer look. "I don't get it. What does 'no maternal match' mean?'"

"It's saying your mother isn't even related to you!"

I shook my head, stunned. "That can't be! Mom always says I'm their miracle child."

"Did she ever actually say she'd given birth to you?" Draya asked.

I thought. "No. She said I arrived long after they'd given up on having a baby. But she also told me flat-out that I'm not adopted. I can't believe she would lie to me. Mom isn't a liar! I mean, even all those questions about the photos turned out to have a logical explanation."

I leaned in again. "Wait! What does the test say about a paternal match? I mean, Dad has to be my real dad. I look just like him!"

Draya shook her head. "He isn't your dad either. But you are a partial match. That means he's at least related to you."

I slumped, fighting back tears. "Then who are my parents? Who am I?"

Draya bit her bottom lip, obviously trying not to blurt an answer.

"What? You know something."

Draya sat staring at the screen. "You know the answer too. Someone related to your dad is your parent. We know now he has a half-sister. I think we can assume she is your mother. Maybe your parents were given custody of you if she was into drugs or even died."

"Then you think that man at the art exhibit was telling the truth? I'm his child, and my name is Summer?"

"April was in a relationship with him, so it's possible." Draya paused, meeting my gaze. "Are you okay? I know this has to be upsetting to you."

"You mean the fact that everything I believed true about myself is a lie?" Sarcasm tinged my words.

"Not everything. You have two parents who love you whether or not they are your birthparents."

"Except they told me to my face I wasn't adopted. And my parents just aren't the type to lie. You know them. They are always about doing the right thing." I jumped to my feet. "I can't believe this! Maybe the DNA test was wrong. Maybe they mixed up the results."

Draya shook her head. "There are protocols to make sure that doesn't happen. Besides, this makes sense with everything else we've found out. Your mom said you came along after they'd given up on having a child. She never specifically said she gave birth to you. And your parents also told you that your dad's half-sister and her boyfriend were into drugs and took off when you were a baby. And that they looked for her but never found any trace of her. So if this April was your birth mom, then maybe your parents became your guardian after your birth mom disappeared."

"So my parents are technically my aunt and uncle. And the change of last name? The fact that Tim and Patty Collins don't actually exist? If it's as easy as my parents getting guardianship, why all the mystery? Why hide those photos? Or change my own name if it was originally Summer? Why be so obsessive about staying off the internet? And why not just tell me the truth to begin with? It isn't as though I'd think less of my parents knowing I was adopted."

Draya shrugged. "Maybe they were going to tell you eventually when they thought you'd be ready for it. Perhaps they didn't want you to know your birth parents were into drugs. Maybe even died of a drug overdose since they never turned up."

"That's a lot of maybes and perhapses." A sudden thought crossed my mind, sending a shiver through me. "That man at the exhibit said he was my birth father. If that's true, he didn't die of an overdose. So where would he have been all these years? And he asked where my mom was. Why would he ask if she was dead?"

"Maybe they split up, and she died afterward."

"But he claimed she'd stolen from him. What would she have stolen?"

Draya looked thoughtful. "If they were both into drugs, maybe she stole drugs from him?"

"And after all these years, he comes back for a few drugs?" I demanded skeptically. "Besides, if he is still alive and she is still alive, where have either of them been all these years? Dad said he searched for his sister and could never find her. Or do you think he was lying about that? None of it explains why they would need to hide having me. Or what happened to my birth parents. Or why Dad would have a different name on his uniform."

"Well, I could bring up the witness protection program again," Draya said thoughtfully. "I mean, just think about it. Maybe your birth parents weren't just into drugs themselves. Maybe he was a dealer. You know, like the cartels. And your parents testified against the cartel, so they had to go into hiding in case the cartel came after them to get revenge."

"Except Dad already told me they weren't in witness protection just like Mom told me I wasn't adopted. So either that isn't true, or my parents are both liars and my birth parents are drug dealers. Either way, everything I ever believed about myself is a lie. And what does that say about me if I'm the daughter of either liars or drug dealers?"

"Hey, hey!" Draya suddenly reached out and wrapped her arms around me in a tight hug. "Don't pay any attention to anything I just said. That was just my imagination going crazy. Besides, even if any of it was true, that doesn't say anything about who you are. Nothing about you has changed. You're the same person you were before all this began."

I sighed. "This is unbelievable. I wish we could go back in

time and not go on that field trip and see those photos. I want my previous boring life back. What am I supposed to do now?"

"I don't know," Draya said. "I'll help you anyway I can. At least until I leave for Sri Lanka. But I really think you should talk to your parents. They're the same people they were before too, and you know they love you. They may have a logical explanation just as they did for the photos."

"I can't tell them we did a DNA test behind their backs." I tried to think, but my mind was a blur. "Besides, what could they say that would change the truth that everything I've ever believed about our family is a lie—even if they didn't technically lie to me?"

"I know. I'm sorry you have to go through this. We seem to be at a dead end about your dad's military service or your parents' last name or the creep claiming to be your birth father. Let me try one more search for Ashlyn Meadowbrook. Maybe I can do a search of New York databases since she appears to live in New York City now."

I sat in silence for several minutes as Draya typed on her tablet while muttering to herself. Finally she stopped and spoke. "Well, that's interesting."

Instantly, I was on alert. "What?"

"According to a New York art magazine, Ashlyn is holding an exhibit at a gallery in New York beginning this coming week."

"Wish we could go to New York for the exhibit. We might be able to find answers. Somehow adventure camp doesn't sound appealing anymore."

"I doubt your parents would let you go to New York City," Draya said.

"Probably not, but it might be my only way to get answers," I countered. "So far nothing they've led me to believe my whole life is true. At least I know now why Dad told me to drop the investigation. The worst is that he told me to trust him and Mom that they had good reasons for not answering my questions. How does any of this counts as good reasons? I love my parents, but shouldn't they have told me the truth?"

My mind whirled as conflicting emotions collided. I wish I hadn't found out all I had. But now that I knew what I did, I couldn't merely ignore it. I needed answers. Real answers. And with clarity of mind, I knew what I had to do. And it had to happen now.

CHAPTER SIXTEEN

"I'm going to New York City."

Draya's eyes widened at my statement. "You can't simply take off for New York. Why don't you talk to your parents again. Tell they what you've found out. Explain how you feel."

"So they can misdirect me again?" I demanded. "If there is a reasonable explanation as to why my parents aren't really my parents, they should have told me long ago. Or even when all of this started. They told me to my face that Dad's sister took those pictures, then ran off and never came back. And they knew that man was telling the truth about being my birth father. They could have explained then about how they ended up with custody of me. I'd have understood if my birth parents were into drugs and couldn't raise a kid. Instead they told me to stop asking questions like I was the one with the problem. I'm not going to give them a chance to just tell me to drop it again. If they won't give me answers, I'll find them myself."

"Well, I'm not saying that's the best idea," Draya said cautiously. "But if you're determined to go to New York City, at least let me help. For one, you do know you're going to need some ID that lets you travel without an adult. And what kind of cash do you have for travel expenses? And do you even know where to stay in New York? Or how to get to this exhibit? And how are you planning to keep your parents from finding out that you aren't at camp?"

She was right, I admitted to myself. I didn't have the slightest idea what I was doing. "Fine. I'd appreciate the help. But only if you let me pay back any costs. And you can't let Reese know. He's already having a hard time with his dad. If I know him, he'd dump his job no matter what the consequences and insist on coming along. This is my problem to deal with, and I don't want anything coming back on him."

Draya and I spent the remainder of the afternoon working out details. Enough students from our high school attended the adventure camp every summer that a bus picked up campers at the school Monday morning and dropped them back off Saturday after camp ended. My parents were planning to drop me off at school before heading to the shop. Instead of boarding the bus, Draya would pick me up in an Uber and take me to the Greyhound station, where I would catch a bus to New York City.

"And you don't think the camp is going to contact my parents when I don't show up? It's not enough to get away. I need to keep them from freaking out and calling the police."

"Not a problem," Draya said calmly. "All I need is the confirmation email you got registering you at camp. Your mom emailed you a copy when she got it, and I've already pulled it up from your email account."

Which meant she'd used my password to get into my email from her laptop. I guess the world was fortunate Draya was on the side of the angels as I hated to think what she could do if she ever decided to use her mad computer skills for anything illegal.

"I'm also working on getting you a state ID that makes you eighteen. Don't ask where I'm getting it. Short story, remember my friend who went to Navy bootcamp in Chicago last year? His senior year he ran around with a pretty wild crowd, and he asked if he could use my mom's laminator and high resolution printer to make fake IDs for him and a couple buddies to get into bars. I was curious how he did the graphics, so I snuck him in to use the printer and laminator in exchange for the program he used to create the IDs. Not my most law-abiding hour, I'll admit. Funny thing is, he is working toward a career in Navy intelligence now."

She hit enter on her keyboard. "Okay, I've used the same photo as on your school ID. I'll run it off and bring it to you when I pick you up tomorrow. It won't have a real ID number, so I'm not even going to try to book you a ticket online. But you should be able to buy a bus ticket at the Greyhound station. Try to time yourself so the ticket attendant is really busy. They'll pay less attention to your ID that way. I've also emailed you a list of youth hostels near the bus station once you get to New York."

While Draya worked, I was busy packing my backpack as though I was leaving for camp. "But how am I going to pass for eighteen? If anything, people usually think I'm younger than I am."

"Act confident. You can get away with most anything if you act like you know what you're doing." Draya shut her laptop. "Now, the good thing is your parents won't be expecting to hear from you once you're at camp since you aren't supposed to be using your phone. So you'll have most of a week before they start worrying. That should be it except getting you some cash. I've got a stash of dollars at home I withdrew to take on this trip. I'll bring that to you tomorrow."

"But—" I started to protest, but she raised her hand to cut

me off.

"I know. I know. It's all too much. You insist on paying me back. That's fine, and I know you will. But I won't be able to get on that plane and enjoy my vacation without knowing you're going to be okay. So just let me do this, okay?"

She let out a sigh. "I hope I'm not crazy for helping you. I wish you'd at least tell Reese."

"There's nothing he can do," I said stubbornly. "I'll tell him when I'm safely back."

"Well, at least keep in touch," Draya responded. "You can count on me as your tech support until I leave. And even then, I'll be in another country, not another planet. My phone will still work if you need me."

I woke up Monday morning surprised I'd slept the night before. Excitement and panic tangoed in me. Today I was running away from the only home I'd known in hopes of finding out my true identity. A tinge of guilt ran through me as I hugged my parents goodbye in the high school parking lot where a couple dozen other students and their parents were exchanging either tearful or excited goodbyes. The bus was already there, and a couple of faculty volunteers were helping students check their luggage in with the bus driver to be stored in the cargo compartment.

I spotted Draya in the crowd, but she stayed away until my parents had left. I made my way over to her, and we drifted casually away from the excited mob of students and parents before one of those faculty volunteers should notice I wasn't checking into the bus. If I had any doubts about taking my search to New York City, what happened next settled it for me.

Draya had slipped me a fat envelope and an ID that looked just like those that came from the DMV. I'd slid the first into my backpack and was stuffing the second into a pocket when Draya pulled out a folded sheet of paper. "I didn't know if you had this, so I printed out the announcement about Ashlyn's exhibit. It has the address in case you need it."

"Oh, Draya, you think of everything!" I impulsively hugged her. "I don't know what I'd do without you."

Just then, I stiffened as over her shoulder I caught a hard, narrowed stare directed my way. My first thought was that one of the faculty volunteers had noticed one of the campers wasn't checking in as she should be. Then I recognized the man who owned that stare. Suddenly dizzy with fear, I spun around so that my backpack blocked his view of my face.

Draya grabbed my arm. "Bailey, what is it?"

"Over there!" I whispered. "The man standing just past the bus near the front steps. That's the man from the art exhibit. The one who claimed to be my father!"

"Are you sure?" Draya asked.

"Yes, of course! Just look at him! He looks like the picture I took. No, don't turn around. He'll know I saw him. How did he find me? There were at least five other schools there. And how would he know I'd be here today?"

I was practically hyperventilating with fear. Taking me by the arm, Draya steered me back toward the group crowded around the bus, following a trajectory that quickly put the bus between us and the man.

"Hey, it's going to be okay. The guy probably found out all the schools that were there and has been checking them one by one. As to being here today, I'm sure that's coincidence. He wouldn't necessarily know school was out for the summer. Since he doesn't know your name, he won't have any way of finding out that you're a student here. At least so long as we get out of here before he sees us."

"I don't know if that's true!" I said tensely. "Look! He's coming over! And he—look! Didn't he just show the bus driver his cell-phone? I told you I thought he'd taken a picture of me. If he shows that around, someone is going to recognize me and tell him who I am."

The bus driver wouldn't recognize me, and I'd never had either of the two faculty volunteers as a teacher. But if the man showed a photo of me to enough students, especially those who'd been at adventure camp last summer with me and Reese, someone was going to give him my name. And with a town as small as ours, it wouldn't be long until he located me.

Draya gave me a comforting pat. "Hey, let me deal with this. He never saw me, remember? I was in the restroom when it all happened. So you just hang back out of sight, and I'll go find out what he's doing."

I did what Draya said, ducking behind the cover of a trio of boys I recognized as ninth-graders who were clowning around posing for selfies. Draya walked straight up to the man. When she said something, he held out his phone. She looked at it, then shook her head emphatically.

She was turning away when disaster struck. I hadn't even realized I was still holding the printout of Ashlyn's exhibit until one of the clowning ninth graders bumped into me—hard! I staggered back, losing my grip on the paper. A gust of wind sent it skittering across the parking lot to where Draya had stepped away from the man. Clearly recognizing it, Draya bent to grab the paper. But the man reached it first.

Picking it up, he started to hand the paper to Draya, then glanced at it. A calculating expression crossed his face as he read it. He turned and surveyed the crowd of students and parents. I knew he couldn't see me behind the boys, but it felt as though he was looking straight at me.

Then Draya snatched the paper from him and walked over to a group of students, where she began chatting and smiling, her back turned to where she knew I was standing. The man didn't bother showing his phone to anyone else but walked over to a small black car. Climbing in, he drove off.

I tried to convince myself I'd imagined the expression on his face. That he'd been fooled by Draya's insistence that the girl in the photo didn't go to this school or live in this town. That he probably hadn't even noticed the subject of Draya's printout. That this was the last time I'd see the man.

But I wasn't convinced because deep down I knew we'd meet again.

CHAPTER SEVENTEEN

There were no more issues in getting away from the school. Campers were now boarding the bus and parents drifting off to the parking lot. No one paid any attention as Draya and I meandered through the cars. Once out of sight of the bus, we headed down the street a couple blocks, where Draya called an Uber.

The driver hardly looked at us as I hoisted my backpack and camera bag into the back seat and we climbed in after them. Draya directed the driver to the Greyhound station. We were just walking in when my phone rang. I looked at the screen, dreading to see one of my parents popping up on Caller ID. Had I come this far only to get caught?

But it was Reese. Before I could let it go to voicemail, Draya nodded at the phone. "You should answer it. He knows you're getting on the bus about now, so he'll keep calling if there's no answer. If he thinks you're safe at camp, he won't bother you the rest of the week."

As always, her logic was flawless. I tapped the screen, "Hi, Reese."

"Hey, I just wanted to touch base before they take your phone away. I wish I was going with you."

"Thanks. I wish you were too. How is it going with your first day of work?"

Reese grunted. "So far not bad. The new building project just broke ground. My first assignment is with the crew stacking and moving debris. Not a bad workout if I can't be playing soccer. Anyway, call me when you get your phone back Friday."

We talked for a few more minutes, then said goodbye and ended the call. Draya accompanied me into the bus station. I had no problem buying a ticket, mainly because the place was so crowded and the ticker clerk so harried he barely glanced at my ID.

I'd chosen the first departure heading the right direction. The call to board was sounding by the time I'd pocketed my ticket and was shouldering my backpack and camera bag. Draya walked me outside to the parked buses, talking non-stop.

"Be sure to get in line right away so you're at the front. And don't follow everyone to the back of the bus. Most trouble takes place at the back. Sit as near the driver as you can."

"Okay, I'll sit near the front," I agreed.

"And keep your carry-on and camera bag with you. The most common theft on buses is theft of carry-ons the owners neglect because they are doing something else."

"Okay. I'll wear my backpack if I get out of my seat."

Draya opened her mouth to say something more, but I interrupted. "You know, you're as bad as my mom."

Draya grinned. "I found a list of precautions for bus travel online, and I didn't want the knowledge to go waste. Most of it's common sense anyway."

"Thanks. I'll stay safe, I promise." I gave her a quick hug, then joined the line of passengers boarding a bus for Toledo, Ohio. The checked luggage was being loaded into a large compartment under the bus, but I didn't have any. My backpack and camera bag would ride with me.

I climbed the bus steps, sure those around me could hear my heart hammering. Any moment, a police officer might clap a hand on my shoulder, demanding to examine my ID. Or even worse, I might see Mom and Dad hurrying up, disappointment on their faces. I didn't even want to think of the man from the exhibit somehow following me from the school to the Greyhound station. *Please let this go well! Don't let me get caught!*

The smell as I stepped aboard the bus distracted me from my fears. My nose wrinkled at a strong whiff of body odor, dirty socks, and fuel. I did my best to inhale shallowly through my mouth, but I could still taste the stale air. Trying to act nonchalant like a seasoned traveler, I slid into the seat directly behind the driver, backpack on my lap and camera bag worn across my body. Draya would be proud of me. I gripped the tiny compass Reese had attached to my camera bag strap, rubbing it between my thumb and first finger. Hopefully, it would soon lead me back to Reese as he'd said when he gave it to me.

An elderly woman sat across the aisle from me. She immediately leaned forward in my direction as though trying to strike up a conversation, but I didn't want to talk to anyone. I wouldn't relax until we'd pulled out and were on the road. Pulling earbuds from my backpack, I listened to music to pass the time, slouched low in my seat in case anyone who would recognize me might be taking this bus.

But the bus rumbled from the station without a single familiar face coming aboard. I let out a long, slow breath as I repositioned my camera bag strap around my neck and across my body so the bag itself was under my arm away from anyone.

Now that we were on the way, I pulled out the itinerary and studied it. The bus ride to New York City was almost twenty hours not counting layovers. I'd purchased a ticket only as far Toledo, Ohio. Draya's suggestion just in case I was tracked to the Greyhound station and someone grilled the ticket clerk about my destination.

The bus lurched to a stop at each Greyhound station along the designated route, and passengers got on and off. As the bus approached the Toledo station, it went under a huge walkway, then pulled into an active bus stop. Not only was there an army of buses, but trains were pulling in nearby with a screech of brakes. Would a train have been a better option?

Grabbing my backpack, I moved awkwardly into the aisle, my legs stiff. As I stepped down to get off, my camera bag strap caught on the door release, yanking me backward onto my bottom on the steps. I hurriedly stood, unhooked the offending strap, and exited the bus, my ears and neck warm. I'd been trying to keep from drawing attention to myself as the fewer people who noticed me the better. So much for that!

The elderly woman who'd been seated across the aisle had deboarded right behind me. She continued to follow as I made my way into the station in search of a restroom. She was walking slowly with a distinct limp, but the station was so crowded with a throng of rushing people that my own progress was just as slow. I'd just spotted the door of the women's restroom and was turning that direction when the elderly woman came up alongside me.

"Goodness, dear," she addressed me with a kindly smile. "I

was afraid you weren't going to make it off the bus."

I shrugged, not knowing what to say.

She went on, "You look terribly weighed down, dear. If you want, I'd be happy to watch your bags for you while you use the restroom."

I studied her. What good would an elderly woman be if someone tried to take my backpack? "Thanks, but I'll keep my bags with me."

Her kindly expression grew firm. "Nonsense, dear. I might not be able to run, but I can scream. Shall I demonstrate?"

I hesitated, wanting to get away from her but not wanting to hurt her feelings. Then a hand took my elbow, guiding me forward. A woman's assertive voice spoke. "No, thank you. She'll keep her bags."

"I was only trying to help," the elderly woman protested.

"I bet you were. Help yourself to her camera and money." The voice held a hint of amusement.

"Well I never!" Spinning around, the elderly woman took off across the station, her limp miraculously vanished.

Turning, I found myself face to face with a woman who looked to be somewhere in her early thirties dressed in Boho style, which I could only identify due to Draya's many fashion magazines. She wore a long-sleeved loose blue floral blouse over faded skinny jeans, her low-cut boots the same blue as the shirt. Dark-blonde hair cascaded down her back.

I liked the style. It was a good look for an artist, as I hoped to be one day. I determined to pay more attention to my clothing choices once I got home. Draya would be more than willing to help me with that project.

"Thank you for the help," I said gratefully. "I wasn't sure how to get away from that lady. She was on my bus when I got on."

The woman smiled. "First time traveling alone?"

"Yes. New York City for college," I offered, using the cover story Draya and I had created. "Going early for a summer class."

The woman gave an approving nod. "New York City is a great place. I'm actually headed there myself. But you have to be smart to stay safe. Where are you staying?"

"I have a list of youth hostels."

"Those are usually affordable. There's a nice one I stayed at years back on the west side of Central Park. It's an old house that's been converted into a hostel. An easy name to remember too—something about Central Park. It's one of the safer ones and in a good area."

"Thanks. I'll check it out."

"And you might want to try traveling by train next time. Amtrack is a much better option in my opinion. It's more expensive, but you avoid some of the security issues you can face on a bus. Well, I'd better get going. My train leaves soon."

I headed to the restroom, both my backpack and my camera bag across my body. Afterward, I looked for something to eat. I purchased a hotdog combo, surprised by how much it cost. I was even more surprised when I checked Draya's envelope and saw it contained at least a thousand dollars in cash. So this was her idea of vacation spending money? It was more than everything I had in my savings account.

Another reminder of the income gap between my family and my best friend's. I determined to spend as little as possible so I could repay her quickly. But I was also thankful to have a friend so generous and quick to help.

I bought my next bus ticket, this time all the way to New York City. With Draya's cash, I could have sprung for a train ticket as my kindly rescuer had suggested. But I had a feeling my fake ID might be one of the security issues Amtrak might keep a closer eye on than the bus ticket clerk. I had an hour before my bus left, so I walked around taking pictures, including a selfie I sent to Draya.

Once on the bus, I got out my phone and pulled up the list of youth hostels Draya had downloaded. One called Central Park West near the southwest corner of Central Park was on the list. It looked like an old luxury brownstone on its website, so I guessed this might be the one my rescuer at the station had mentioned.

After looking up directions from the bus station to the hostel, I decided to try to sleep in hopes of time passing faster. According to Google, it was only an eleven hour drive from Toledo to New York City. But with all the stops and two transfers, it would be a grand total of twenty-six hours. I groaned at the prospect of being on the bus so long. But the thought of actually finding myself in New York City by late morning tomorrow made me feel both excited and terrified.

CHAPTER EIGHTEEN

The bus finally pulled into the Port Authority Bus Terminal in New York City just short of noon on Tuesday. As I stood up and waited for feeling to come back to my legs, a myriad of emotions ran through me. Excitement. Anxiety. And a lot more I wasn't sure I could name.

After sitting on the bus for so long, I decided to walk from the station to Central Park, which was about twenty blocks northwest of the terminal. My backpack securely fastened by both shoulder straps and waist strap and camera bag across my chest, I set out, trying to take in everything as I walked. People of numerous nationalities streamed by, and I caught bits of conversation from many different languages. The buildings ranged from quaint one-story cafes to looming skyscrapers.

Panic rose up inside me as what I'd done in running away to this alien place began to sink in. Not only had I left the safety of my small Indiana town for one of the busiest cities in the United States, but I was surrounded by literally millions of strangers with no concrete plan of where I was going or how I was going to proceed. My heart raced, and I slowed my pace. A swarm of people passed me on both sides.

Why had I thought I could do this? Why hadn't I begged Reece to defy his dad and come with me? This was different than sitting with my best friends at my kitchen table trying to piece together clues. I should have confronted my parents and demanded answers.

I drew in a slow breath and blew it out. No, that wouldn't have worked. I'd already asked for answers, and my parents had refused to give them. That was why I was here. My life was a lie. I had to find the truth on my own.

This was not the time for panic. I needed to get myself together and focused. I could do this. I had to.

I walked until I arrived at the southwest corner of Central Park by Columbus Circle. Food vendors lined the curb. Everything from kabobs to gyros to ice cream could be purchased from small trucks. Unfamiliar spices tantalized my nose, some of them so strong they made my eyes water. If Reese and Draya were with me, we'd have fun trying the different foods, Draya the most adventuresome of our trio when it came to spicy foods.

Music filled the air, and I momentarily forgot my panic. Detouring toward the sound, I discovered the source. An older man with graying hair and a beard wearing a threadbare corduroy jacket and kilt sat on a bench playing an accordion. My photographer's eye was already composing a picture of him even while I wondered if there were rules about taking photos of people in the park.

I started to approach him, then stopped. He ignored me and kept playing. I took a step closer and lifted my camera. He looked up and nodded sideways with his head. I followed his motion. There was a top hat with coins and bills in it next to him.

Digging into my pocket, I pulled out two one-dollar bills and dropped them in the hat. He nodded at me, and I took that as permission to take photos. Kneeling down, I took full-length photos of him, then focused in on his face and even on the aged hands playing the accordion. I didn't stop until I'd taken at least twenty photos. At this rate I'd need to buy an extra photo memory card soon.

I then continued my journey to the Central Park West youth hostel I'd looked up on the bus. The address took me to an aged single-story brick building that looked just like it had on the website. I climbed the three steps to the door, where I stopped, wondering if I was supposed to just walk in or knock and wait to be let in. While I stood there debating, the door opened and two girls walked out, one tall and blonde, the other petite of some Asian ethnicity. They looked late teens or early twenties. They stopped to scrutinize me, and I wondered from their expressions whether they were thinking I didn't look old enough to be traveling alone.

Finally the tall, blonde girl spoke. "Hi. I'm Holly, and this is Mandy. Are you staying here?"

"I hope to. Do you know if there are any rooms available?"

Holly nodded. "There's a check-in desk in the lobby. Mrs. Perry will get you set up with a room."

Going inside, I approached the check-in desk. I was soon following a middle-aged woman upstairs and down a hall to a small, white room with a three-drawer wooden dresser, desk, and twin bed with a quilted blanket. I peeked into the bathroom, which held an old-fashioned claw tub with a more modern shower attachment added to the wall above the tub.

Mrs. Perry was chattering the entire time. "This building dates from the early 1900s, the home of a railroad baron. It was redesigned as a hotel not long after World War Two. But all the plumbing and electricity were redone just a decade or so back. Follow me, and I'll show you the rest of the facilities."

Mrs. Perry handed me a room key, and I locked the door behind me before following her down the hall to a room that held a flat-screen TV, several sofas, and a scattering of tables and chairs. The room was empty except for two guys playing a game of chess at one table.

"The common room is open from six a.m. to eleven p.m., but no loud noise is permitted after nine p.m. You can store your food in the refrigerator and use the microwave to cook your own meals. Clean up after yourself. All dishes must be washed and returned to the cupboards. If you need anything, come to the front desk. If no one is there, ring the bell."

With that, Mrs. Perry headed back downstairs, and I was on my own again. I returned to my room, where I texted Draya to let her know I had arrived safely. Then I unpacked the few belongings I'd brought. My stomach rumbled, reminding me I hadn't yet eaten. I decided to go back to the corner with the food vendor trucks and get lunch before trying to find the gallery. I had only a few days to get the answers I needed before my parents discovered I wasn't at camp. One more lie in a big web of lies.

It was only a few blocks back to the corner where the food trucks were parked. I smelled them before they came into view. I didn't recognize most of the food choices, but I finally selected a rice and chicken dish with some kind of white sauce that didn't look too spicy. Then I found a bench where I could watch people hurry by as I ate.

My phone rang, startling me. I glanced at it. Draya. I answered it.

"How are you? How is New York?"

I paused before answering. "I'm okay."

"That's it? Okay?"

I hesitated. How could I convey my feelings to Draya? After all, she was getting ready to fly halfway around the world. But no matter where she was, she'd have her parents with her.

"Bailey?"

"Sorry. I think I'm a bit intimidated by the busyness of the city. I wish you and Reese were with me. I've never done anything like this before, especially not alone."

"Do you regret your choice? It would be easy enough to contact your parents and come home. In fact—"

"In fact what?"

"Your dad called me today!"

CHAPTER NINETEEN

My stomach clenched. "You're kidding! Does he know I'm here? What did he say?"

"No, he thinks you're safely at camp," Draya assured me hastily. "He just wanted to know what search engines I used to find the information about Ashlyn."

I relaxed. "That makes sense. He told me he was trying to find out how this woman had photos of me."

"Well, maybe he's trying to search for her on his own. Whatever that DNA report, he's your dad and has to be worried about you. Especially after seeing that picture of the guy who is probably your birth father."

I sighed. "Maybe I should have warned my parents he was in town."

"I won't argue with that," Draya responded. "I still think you should just talk to them. But I don't think you need to worry. If he'd tracked you to your parents by now, your dad would be asking me about more than tracking down Ashlyn Meadowbrook. And since it's been more than twenty-four hours, I figure he must have left town already or he would have found your parents by now. I mean, it was Ashlyn Meadowbrook he was looking for, right? To find whoever took those pictures? And he couldn't know for sure you're the baby in those photos. So he probably gave up on looking for you and went back to looking for her."

I wished I was as optimistic about that. On the other hand, if I was right that he'd noticed the PR for Ashlyn's exhibit on that printout, then he might have decided to do exactly what I was doing—head to New York City and look for that gallery.

"I'm actually getting ready now to head over to *The Light Room*, the gallery hosting Ashlyn's exhibit," I said. "I'm hoping she might have some information on my birth mom since April was in some of the photos that looked like they were taken by the same photographer."

That my birth dad might have the same goal was a possibility I didn't add. Draya didn't need more worry about me to spoil her vacation. I would just have to keep a sharp eye out for the man from the exhibit.

"That sounds promising," Draya responded cheerfully. "I fly out first thing in the morning, so be sure to call tonight and let me know how it goes."

I checked the address for the gallery on Google maps. It was on the west side of Central Park but almost four miles north of the youth hostel. I wasn't about to walk that far. My choices were to go by city bus or the subway. I headed to the nearest subway station, and was relieved to see the ticket machines had a variety of options for both bus and subway. I ended up purchasing the seven-day MetroCard, which would allow me unlimited use of both subway and city buses for a week.

Going by bus would allow me to see more of the city, so I located the closest bus stop and boarded the first north-bound bus. I settled into a window seat near the front as I had on the bus from Indiana. The bus pulled onto Central Park West, heading north. Trees obscured the view of Central Park on one side of the street, and tall buildings lined the other. Once past Central Park, buildings lined both sides of the street.

Movement out the window caught my attention. A group of teen boys were playing basketball on a court sporting cracks and a few potholes. The players easily maneuvered around the holes.

Bright-colored street art on the side of the building next to them captured my attention. The word "Created" was drawn in an elongated 3D street art style with shades of blue merging into purple. Stars appeared to be shooting out from it. The words "In Christ Jesus" were written in smaller letters underneath.

Before I could see more, we were past it. My mind raced. Was this the same street art Ashlyn had photographed? It definitely looked the same to me, but I needed to know for sure. I would have to find it later and look at it close up. Unfortunately, I hadn't noticed any of the street names or even what kind of building sported the artwork. I'd only noticed the basketball court.

Why hadn't I paid more attention to where I was? But it was too late now. For the moment, it was time to concentrate on the finding *The Light Room*. Feeling both tense and restless, I decided to get off several stops before the gallery and walk the rest of the way.

I started down the street, keeping track of the street numbers so I wouldn't miss my destination. I stopped in front of a gallery that displayed a painting of a pond filled with lily pads on an easel in the front window. I peered inside. Large white walls held only one or two paintings each, all with the same lily pad theme woven through them in a style I could only describe as playful. I'm sure they were supposed to have some deeper meaning, but it was lost on me. I glanced at the gallery sign. This wasn't *The Light Room*.

Sweet smells coming from a bakery with a green and white awning drew me, but I pushed on, determined to find the gallery I was looking for. A small shopping mall and takeout places offering a variety of foods lined my route before I stopped in front of a white building that looked like it had once been a private home. A hand-painted sign read *The Light Room*. An "Open" lanyard hung on the door.

I climbed the wide wooden steps to the small porch, then hesitated, suddenly nervous about going inside now that I was here. I peered through the large front window. This gallery was smaller than the other one I'd passed, and I couldn't get a good look at the artwork from outside. I didn't see any customers inside or anyone at all. Which made this a perfect opportunity to approach the gallery staff with my questions.

Taking a deep breath, I reached for the doorknob. Just then two people walked into view. I bit back a gasp and stepped out of line of sight from the front window, my heart pounding. The angle still allowed me a view of the two people inside as they crossed the floor. One was a woman with white hair arranged in a stylish knot, carefully applied makeup, and wearing a trendy pantsuit. She was in conversation with a blue-eyed, brown-haired man I immediately recognized. It was the stranger who'd been showing my picture around. The one who claimed to be my birth father. This was what I'd feared since I'd seen him snatch up the printout of Ashlyn's exhibit yesterday morning in the parking lot.

I forced myself to take a calming breath. Neither had seen me yet. My supposed father was talking with the woman, smiling and chatting. Did he know her, or was he using charm to get the information he wanted? In my previous encounters at the art exhibit in Chicago and when he'd shown up at my school, he hadn't appeared friendly and chatty but instead creepy and even threatening.

The man turned away from the woman and began walking toward the door. In moments, we would be face to face. I fled down the stairs. Rushing around the side of the gallery, I positioned myself as flat as I could against the wall, hoping the man wouldn't walk my way.

The door shut, and steps grew closer. I froze, holding my breath, as he passed within yards of me, never glancing my way.

I sagged against the building. Hiding in the shadow of the gallery, I was uncertain of my next move. And more importantly, uncertain of whether I was in danger or not. Was the man indeed a drug dealer, or had Draya's imagination gone wild? What did a drug dealer even look like? Maybe he really was just looking for a former girlfriend who'd stolen something of value from him.

Still, I couldn't forget the conversation I'd overheard between my parents. Overprotective or not, they'd been genuinely worried when they'd seen this man's photo. And maybe he wasn't anything as dramatic as a drug dealer, but I had no reason to doubt their word that the man had been a drug user when they'd known him.

I took a deep breath and released it. I'd come to New York for answers, and if nothing else, this man would have them. I decided to follow him but play it safe and stay out of sight. I waited until the man was a good half-block ahead of me, then stealthily fell into step behind him.

CHAPTER TWENTY

The man boarded a bus. It was packed with people, so I followed, keeping my head down in hopes he wouldn't notice me. Thankfully, he made his way to the back of the bus. I took the first available seat and kept a close eye on passengers getting on and off at each stop, not wanting to miss the man when he got off.

When we reached the east side of Central Park, the man joined a group of people filing off the bus. I took my place at the end of the line. Once off the bus, I followed, hanging back behind several other passengers until I confirmed he was heading into Central Park. The park was crowded with sightseers, so it wasn't difficult to stay close behind him without being seen if he glanced back.

All was going well when the man disappeared behind a large castle with a sign announcing that it was named Belvedere Castle. Just then a group of Asian tourists following the raised pennant of their guide pushed in front of me, blocking the man from my view. By time I got around them, there was no sight of him. I rounded the castle at a run, determined not to lose him.

In my haste, I didn't pay attention to where I was going. A loud shout startled me. I looked up into the panicked eyes of a bicyclist headed straight toward me. Though he made an effort to swerve, it was too late. A moment later, I was on the ground tangled with the bicycle and its rider.

Pain pulsed through me. I pushed to a sitting position, my head throbbing. The bicyclist, a young man not much older than myself, scrambled to his feet and looked down at me, worry in his eyes. "You okay? You ran right in front of my bicycle. I couldn't stop."

I stared up at him, trying to make sense of his words. The bicyclist offered me his hand, and I let him pull me to my feet. My ankle throbbed almost as much as my head. I put my hand to my head, and it came away bloody. This wasn't good.

"It wasn't your fault. Don't worry about it," I said. I was relieved the bicyclist appeared unhurt as I was well aware he had every right to blame me or even charge me for his bike if it was damaged. He gave me a doubtful look, then picked up his bicycle and remounted. If there was any damage, it wasn't enough to keep him from riding off.

"Here. Hold this against the wound to stop the bleeding." A white handkerchief appeared in front of my face. Taking it gratefully, I pressed it to my bloody head. Only then did I realize who had handed it to me. The man claiming to be my father. I spun around, pain shooting through my ankle as I poised to flee.

"Don't go," the man said urgently. "I won't harm you. I only want to talk to you. My name is Martin Beck. I'm your father."

Pressing the white cloth to my head, I took two steps back. "What do you want?" I hated the tremble in my voice.

"Why do I have to want something to talk to my own child? Are you afraid?"

I opened my mouth to say something, but nothing would come out.

"Summer? Are you okay?"

My knees felt weak, and I sank to the lush green lawn, ignoring his use of the name Summer. "I'm not sure what to believe."

He knelt beside me. "Did your uncle tell you I was a monster? A drug dealer who got sent to prison?"

There was an edge to his tone that made me uncomfortable and anxious. Why hadn't I at least left my parents a note telling them where I was going and why? Or messaged Reese? If anything happened to me, only Draya knew where I was, and she was leaving for Sri Lanka in the morning.

"Your uncle would say anything to turn you against me," Martin went on. "Tim never liked me. I've missed you."

I was confused. "What about the accusation you made at the college art gallery? About my mom stealing from you and hiding me?"

"Listen, why don't we go somewhere and talk. You need answers, and I have them."

"I can't," I stammered. "I have to get back."

I stood and started to walk, limping heavily on my injured ankle. Martin fell into step beside me. "Get back to where, Summer? Aren't you here on your own? Trying to find your birth mom the same as I am?"

I stopped and stared at him. "My birth mom? She's here? How do you know? When we met at the exhibit, you didn't know where she was."

"True. And I realized by the look on your face you had no idea what I was talking about. Never knew I existed. I had to find you again. Let you know I'd have never abandoned my baby girl if you hadn't been so cruelly stolen from me."

I knit my eyebrows together. "But you said you were sent to prison. If you were in prison, how could you have taken care of me?"

His face darkened, eyes narrowed. "I have either your uncle or April to blame for my time in prison. I've been looking for you and your mom since I got out. I might never have located either of you if I hadn't seen your picture on an advertisement for that exhibit in Chicago. And when I saw that paper your friend dropped, I knew I'd find April here in New York. It was always her dream to come here and be a big-shot artist. I just never figured I'd find you here too.

I had dropped the paper, not Draya, if that mattered. I stayed silent, fearing his anger but at the same time utterly confused. It must have shown because he answered my unspoken question.

"The notice of the art exhibit. The artist was Ashlyn Meadowbrook, same as the artist who exhibited all those baby pictures of you in Chicago. You think I didn't guess that girl was your friend after she looked at your picture and swore up and down you didn't attend that school, then just happened to have a flyer advertising the same artist clear on the other side of the country? The exhibit's why I'm here. Isn't the same true for you?"

"This Ashlyn Meadowbrook," I finally managed to get out cautiously. "Are you saying she's a friend of April? That she knows where to find April?"

"If I'm right," the man said flatly, "April and Ashlyn are one and the same."

I stepped back, shaking my head. He stepped forward, so

close I could feel his breath on my face. He went on. "I was with April when she took some of those photos that were in the exhibit. So either April is Ashlyn or the woman you know as Ashlyn stole the portraits from April. That's not very likely. Think about it, Summer."

"Bailey. My name is Bailey."

His eyes narrowed, his voice hardening. "I named you Summer. They not only took you but stole your whole identity."

"Who did?"

"Your kidnappers. The people you know as Tim and Patty Collins."

"They didn't kidnap me." Anger at his accusation erased the anxiety plaguing me.

"Then why did they change their names and yours and move from Chicago to Nowheresville rural Indiana?"

"I don't know. But I know my parents. There has to be an explanation."

"And yet you're here on your own searching for April. Or are you telling me it's just a coincidence, and you're just some sort of groupie for this Ashlyn Meadowbrook."

My phone rang. I glanced at it. Draya. I hurriedly answered. "I'm in Central Park with Martin Beck, the man claiming to be my father."

If he did something to me, at least Draya would know where I last was and that I was with Martin.

"Are you okay?"

"I am so far." I turned back to Martin and said harshly, "I'm leaving, and you'd better not follow me or come near me again or I'll have my friend here call 911. She's going to stay on the line with me, so if you try anything I'll scream bloody murder, then she can call 911, and we'll see if there are any police officers around here. If I have to, I'll tell them you are the reason my head is bleeding and that you are trying to kidnap me."

Another lie I never wanted to tell. But hopefully, I wouldn't have to follow through on that threat. Holding the phone to my ear with one hand while holding the bloody handkerchief to my head with the other, I turned and began hobbling through the park toward the nearest exit, my ankle throbbing. Was Martin following me?

I glanced back. He stood, arms crossed, staring after me. Though relieved he'd taken me at my word, I feared I hadn't seen the last of him.

CHAPTER TWENTY-ONE

Of course, Draya had heard everything I'd just said. She was venting into the phone before I could get far enough away to respond. "Bailey, are you sure you're okay? I can call 911. Maybe I should just to be safe."

"No, that really isn't necessary. I was just—well, bluffing." As I headed toward an exit on Central Park West, I filled Draya in on Martin's accusations. "So he says my parents kidnapped me, changed our names, and moved us to Nowheresville, Indiana. And the thing is, from everything we've found out, what he said appears to be true."

"Maybe. But you have to think about motive," Draya argued back. "If it's true, why did your parents do it? They love you. No doubt about that. They would never do anything to harm you. I hate to keep repeating myself, but why don't you call and ask them why they did it. You're going to have to do some explaining either way. So you might as well get it over with."

"I...I wouldn't know what to say. And I only have a few days until they are going to arrive at camp to pick me up and find out I'm not there. Right now I'm still processing the fact that I appear to have a drug-dealing felon for a birth father and a drug-using birth mother who may or may not be dead. I certainly can't imagine she's a successful artist going by the name Ashlyn Meadowbrook, no matter what Martin Beck says."

"Who your birth parents are and what they have done in the

past has nothing to do with who you are. Remember when we first saw the wall art photo on Ashlyn's artist page? 'Created in Christ Jesus.' Reese said that means we are created by God to do good things. Who your birth parents are isn't going to change that."

"You believe what Reese said? Honestly?"

There were a few moments of silence, and I wondered if I'd lost connection. Then Draya spoke. "I'm starting to. I'd rather believe in a God who has a plan for us than believe everything happens by chance. If there is no plan for us, then where's the motivation to be a better person? To help others? Or to be unselfish and generous?" She paused before asking, "Does that make sense?"

"It does. I've never thought about it before this whole mystery with my baby photos. I've always gone to church with my parents, but I guess it's never really been personal for me."

"But it is to Reese, and I'm starting to believe he's right." Draya stopped talking, and the sound of voices near her reached me. Then she resumed our call. "Sorry, but I have to go now. My mom is hurrying me to finish up my packing."

We said goodbye, and I headed back to the youth hostel. With my injuries, it might have been smarter to take a bus. But walking gave me a better chance to process the day's events. Thankfully, no one was in the front lobby when I entered, and I was able to get to my room without being noticed.

Catching a glimpse of myself in a mirror above the dresser, I saw a large bruise on one cheek and several scratches to add to my catalog of injuries. I decided the best cure would be to soak in a hot bath, a pointer I'd learned from Reese, who as an athlete routinely endured bruising and sprains. While I relaxed in the antiquated claw-foot tub, I replayed everything that had happened. Seeing Martin talking to the woman in the gallery. Was she the owner? An employee? Ashlyn Meadowbrook herself?

Then my stealth pursuit of Martin Beck through Central Park. Getting hit by a bicycle. The ensuing conversation with Martin. Was Martin right about Ashlyn and April being the same person? He could be telling the truth about being with April when she took the pictures. After all, I'd found pictures that had me with both Martin and April. So we'd been a family of sorts at one time. What had happened to change things?

More importantly, what would Martin do if he found April? Every encounter with him had left me confused and anxious. If she'd really stolen from him, she needed to know he was looking for her. Or even if she hadn't but he believed she did. Either way, if Martin really was a felon drug-dealer and believed April had double-crossed him as he'd suggested, she could be in danger from him.

Still, one other thing kept coming back to me. My parents believed April to be dead. By their account—which I certainly trusted more than Martin's—they'd searched for her for years without finding her. How did that fit into all this? And what about Martin's suggestion that my parents might have something to do with him going to prison?

I had more questions now than before and few answers.

Climbing out of the tub, I toweled off and pulled on a soft athletic outfit. My phone showed it was eight p.m., and I hadn't eaten since lunch. Dropping onto the bed, I shut my eyes, planning to rest a few minutes before finding something to eat. Next thing I knew, I was waking up to sunlight streaming in a window. I'd slept through dinnertime until morning.

My phone stopped ringing, then started again. That must have been what finally awoke me. I reached to get the phone from where it had fallen from my bed to the floor. Everything hurt, and a groan escaped me as I finally grabbed up the phone.

It was Draya. "We're getting ready to leave for the airport."

I forced myself to sound cheerful. "I hope you have a great flight and enjoy the summer with your relatives."

I did hope that, but I also didn't want her to go. She was my lifeline. She was also the only one who knew where I was.

"I will. But—" There was silence on her end.

"What aren't you telling me?"

"It's just—"

"Tell me."

"Well, last night Reese told his dad he was taking the rest of the week off no matter what his dad said. Then he arrived at the camp first thing this morning to surprise you."

"Oh no! Does he know I'm here?"

"He called me the minute he found out you weren't there." The hesitant way Draya spoke made me certain she was afraid I'd be angry with her answer. I knew my best friend too well not to read between the lines. She'd told him, all right!

"It's okay," I assured her. "If you hadn't told him, he would have called my parents. That would have been even worse. Was he angry?"

"At first. I had to tell him about the DNA test and Martin showing up at the school to explain just why this trip to New

York was so important to you. He was torn between being hurt we hadn't informed him and a bit angry we'd left him out of it."

"Did you explain we didn't want to worry him when he already had problems with his dad to deal with?"

"I did. He said, and I quote, 'What good is having a boyfriend if you don't let them help you when you need it.' End quote."

I groaned.

"Reese will come around," Draya said consolingly. "He was upset we hadn't included him in any of it. He sounded concerned for your safety too."

"Yeah, well, it's not like there was anything he could have done to help me. Not worth getting his dad all angry with him. I can't believe he ditched his job to drive to camp."

"Yeah, well, maybe he thinks you're worth getting his dad mad. Hey, Mom is giving me her hurry-up sign. I have to leave now. Stay safe."

I nodded, then realized she couldn't see me. Aloud, I said, "I will."

I hoped I was telling the truth. But how safe was I—or April— if Martin didn't get the answers he wanted? Because if he was right and she and Ashlyn Meadowbrook were one and the same, then my dad's little sister was very much alive even if my parents thought otherwise.

CHAPTER TWENTY-TWO

A bagel and a bottle of water later, I was back on the bus headed to *The Light Room*. Although my ankle was tender and my head still hurt, I was ready. I had my phone out and set to video while I watched for the place where I'd seen the basketball players and street art yesterday.

This time as the bus approached the neighborhood, the basketball court was empty, and I almost missed the colorful Created graphic on a brick wall bordering the basketball court. I hit the video button just in time. Watching my phone as it recorded, I realized the brick building next to the basketball court had a square tower with a spire on top rising from the roof. It was narrow and antiquated like something from the colonial era, but when I replayed the video, I realized it must be a church steeple.

That made sense with the artwork being a Bible verse. After I checked out the Ashlyn Meadowbrook exhibit at the gallery and found out what I could about the artist, maybe I'd take the bus back and see if there was anyone at the church who could tell me about the street art.

Getting off the bus at a stop close to the gallery, I walked the remaining block to *The Light Room*. The "Open" lanyard was on the door. Climbing the steps, I crossed the small porch and eased the door open. A woman stood in the large entry room, her back to the door, long, dark-blonde hair spilling down over her shoulders. Turning to face me, she said warmly, "Welcome to *The Light Room*. Is this your first time visiting us?"

To my astonishment, I recognized the gallery host the moment I saw her face and heard her voice. She was the woman in Boho-style dress who'd scared off my would-be bag-snatcher in the Toledo terminal on Monday. This time she was wearing a loose flowered dress complimented by large hoop earrings and sandals. She looked at home in the middle of all this art.

"It's you!" I exclaimed. "I never expected to see you again. Certainly not here. Thanks for recommending that youth hostel."

She smiled, then leaned forward to study my bruised, scratched face. "I was worried about you after that incident in Toledo with the phony lady trying to pass herself off as a sweet old grandmother. It looks like I worried for good reason. What happened?"

I explained that I'd gotten hit by a bike in Central Park.

"Ouch! And this is your first trip to New York City?"

I nodded, which made my head start hurting again. I ignored the pain.

"Then let me welcome you to New York City and this art gallery."

"Are you the manager here? Or the owner?" I thought of the woman I'd seen through the window the day before.

"No, Victoria Claussen is the owner, and she's here most days. She just happens to be out today, so I'm filling in. Did you want a tour of the gallery, or would you rather simply wander through?"

I hesitated. I'd love to wander, but if this woman worked

here, letting her act as my guide might give me opportunity to ask questions about the Ashlyn Meadowbrook exhibit and the artist herself. "I'd love a tour."

With that we were off. The guide gave background on each exhibit, but it was the fourth and last one I was waiting for. Even though I'd expected it, I was still overwhelmed as I stood in front of a wide selection of large prints featuring myself as a baby and toddler, including several that included the blanket and field of daisies. While nowhere as extensive as the Portraits of Summer exhibit in Chicago and featuring smaller prints than had been showcased there, it was still an impressive display of photographic art.

I spoke up. "This is the exhibit I'm most interested in. I love the way the photographer captured the child's facial expressions both as an infant and a toddler."

The woman gave me a sharp look. "It sounds like you know something about photography. I will say I prefer art myself that features people rather than abstract art or even just scenery on its own. Are you interested in the field of photographic art?"

This was just the opening I needed. "Yes, I'm hoping to be a professional photographer myself someday. I just love this artist's work. In fact, I was hoping you might be able to tell me something about the photographer, Ashlyn Meadowbrook. I would love to touch base with her in person. Ask her how she goes about doing an exhibit like this. Does she ever come in here personally?"

But my tour guide was already shaking her head. "Ashlyn's a very private person. She doesn't meet with buyers in person or even exhibit publicly very often. Which is why this is such an exclusive opportunity to acquire her art. This particular exhibit is her tribute to her daughter."

"Her tribute to her daughter?"

A bell jangled, signaling someone else had entered the gallery. The woman turned toward the sound.

Before my chance evaporated, I said in a rush, "I'd really like to meet her. Would it be possible to give me some contact information so I could follow up personally to see if she'd be willing to meet with me?"

The tour guide was now frowning, her headshake even more emphatic. "That is out of the question. I told you she's a very private person. But I would encourage you to come back for her next exhibit, Faces of America, which will be on display next month. The exhibit features close-up photos of faces from babies to senior citizens that demonstrate ethnic diversity as well as a range of emotions. Meanwhile, feel free to walk around and look at the exhibits as long as you like."

With that, she hurried off to greet the newcomers. I stood staring at the photos in front of me. This was a tribute to Ashlyn's child? What did my tour guide mean by a tribute? Weren't tributes for some famous or someone who had died?

Once again, I wasn't getting answers but even more questions. My gut clenched. It was Wednesday. In three more days, my parents would expect me to be on a bus heading home—and no longer out of cell phone communication. My time to find answers was running out!

CHAPTER TWENTY-THREE

I stood in front of the exhibit pondering my next move. The tour guide must know the artist. Or at least the director, Victoria, should know her. But how could I get them to give me that information? Or was there somewhere information was kept I could access undetected? A computer, maybe?

I wished Draya was here. She was more creative than I was when it came to obtaining information. She was also more skilled at research. What would she do? What should I do?

Glancing around, I noticed a door partway open behind the Portraits of Summer exhibit. The tour guide was occupied discussing a photo in the first exhibit with the newcomers. I swiftly moved to the door and peeked in. A large wood desk and file cabinets made clear this must be the gallery office. On the desk were untidy stacks of paper and files as well as a small flatscreen angled so I couldn't see the screen and attached to a laptop.

My heartbeat sped up. Did I dare enter and snoop? Heat burned my face. What had I become I'd even consider trespassing?

That was an easy answer. Someone desperate for the truth. The truth among the thousand lies I'd grown up believing. Somewhere there was a logical explanation, and if that answer meant snooping to find Ashlyn's information, I'd do it. Ironic that the events of these last few weeks had started in my parents' home office snooping for information on my family history, and now I was in another office still snooping with even less answers than when I'd started.

With one more backward glance, I slipped in through the partly open door, wondering what I'd say if I was caught. The truth. After all, that's what I was seeking, so it was only right I tell the truth.

Hurrying around the desk, I saw to my disappointment the computer screen was powered down. I picked up a stack of folders and began rifling through them. They appeared to be contractual agreements about scheduled gallery exhibits between Victoria Claussen, director of *The Light Room*, and various names I assumed to be the artists in question.

I knew I was right when I read the name Ashlyn Meadowbrook and an exhibit named *Summer* in the third file. I flipped a page, and suddenly the air seemed sucked from the room. A small black-and-white image that was part of what looked like a photocopied driver's license stared up at me. An image I recognized.

I forced myself to take a deep breath and blow it back out. This couldn't be right! But no, a closer look didn't change anything. The image was definitely of the woman I'd talked to minutes earlier. And the name on the photocopied ID was Ashlyn Meadowbrook. Whether it was also the photo of April Hill, I couldn't tell. The too-thin girl in her late teens with short, dyed hair I'd seen in my baby pictures looked nothing like this well-groomed professional woman with long, thick dark-blonde hair.

I was starting to hyperventilate. Suddenly, I needed fresh

air. Now. Dropping the file back onto the desk, I turned to exit the office.

"What are you doing in here?" My earlier tour guide stood in the door, all pleasantness now gone from her expression. I clutched at the desk, steadying myself as my legs went weak.

"I asked you a question." Stepping into the office, the woman shut the door behind her. "First, you ask questions about Ashlyn Meadowbrook. Now I find you poking where you don't belong. I'm not sure whether to call Victoria or the police. What were you looking for?"

The police? My voice came out in a squeak. "I wasn't stealing anything, I promise. I was simply looking for information."

"So you said." She took another step forward, her facial features stony. "And what did you think you would find in Victoria's office?"

I took a shaky breath as I picked up the file I'd been scanning. "What I came for." I flipped the file open to the photocopied ID. "That's your picture in this contract file for the Summer exhibit. Why did you lie about your name? Why does everyone lie to me?"

Okay, so my exaggeration sounded like a whining toddler, but my pain was real. Her lips tightened as though she had no intention of answering, but her stony expression softened fractionally. I hurried on. "There's no point denying you are Ashlyn Meadowbrook. So why didn't you tell me when I was asking about the exhibit?"

"When I said the photographer was a private person, I was telling the truth. I don't talk about my private life." Her tone was curt. "Listen, I don't know who you think you are or what it is you want from me. I gave you a suggestion for a youth hostel when we first met because I could tell you were new to traveling alone. Now it feels like you are stalking me."

"I'm not stalking you. At least not for bad reasons." She was starting to turn away. Desperate to get her attention. I blurted out. "As to who I am, that's the problem. I don't know who I am. I'm trying to find out. But one thing I do know. I am the baby in those photos. I met a man named Martin Beck who says he's my birthfather, but I don't if that's true. I do know my birth mother is a woman named April Hill."

I pulled out my phone and swiped to bring up the baby photo I'd found taken with a young April and the man who could be Martin. "See? That's me and my birth parents. So if you really took all those photos, then you must have some idea who you shot the portraits for and where I can find this April Hill. Please, can you help me?"

I don't know what I was expecting. Maybe that she'd burst out with the wonderful news she was really April Hill, throw her arms around me, and tell me she was my mother and had been looking for me my entire life. Or at worst, explain she'd created the exhibit with permission of a photography client, and now that she knew I was her client's daughter, she'd be happy to give me that woman's contact information.

Instead, the look on her face made my heart sink. It was ice-cold and furious. Between gritted teeth, she demanded, "Is this some kind of sick joke? Where did you get that photo? Did Martin Beck put you up to this? Are you dealing for him? You're too young to be one of his girlfriends."

I was stunned at the accusation. "No! Of course not. I'd

never even met him until he saw me at your exhibit in Chicago. I was on a school field trip, and he was there too. He told me he was my birth father and asked if I knew where my birth mother, April Hill, was. I thought it was some kind of mistake. Except I knew it was me in those pictures. Then when I saw him here in New York, I knew he was trying to find the photographer too."

"Martin is here? In New York City?"

I've heard the expression "white as a ghost" often enough. But I never thought it was literal. While Ashlyn didn't turn quite white, she paled considerably. She swayed slightly, then drew herself up tall before speaking through stiff lips. "I don't know what your game is, but this is no longer funny. And you are not the child in that photo—or my exhibit. That child died when she was a toddler. For that matter, so did April Hill. So the only way you could have that photo or that information is from Martin Beck."

A light knock on the door interrupted the conversation. Opening the door, Ashlyn dredged up a smile for one of the women she'd been showing around when I'd ducked in the office. The woman smiled apologetically. "Sorry to bother you, but we're about to leave and wondered if you'd found that online purchasing information you'd mentioned if we decide we'd like to buy some pieces."

"Just a moment, and I'll be right back with you." Ashlyn's smile faded as the woman walked back to join her group. She turned to me. "You need to go now, or I will call the police. But let me say this to you because you are still only a kid and I hate to see a kid walking into a lion's den. Whatever you and Martin Beck are up to, it can only be something ugly and dangerous, and it will only end up in disaster. So if you don't want to end up like—well, like April Hill, I'd suggest getting out while you still can. And don't try contacting me again. Or come back to this gallery because believe me, you won't find me here again."

She gestured me toward the door. Heat rising up my neck and ears, I exited the office, pushed by the group of tourists, and all but ran out of the gallery.

CHAPTER TWENTY-FOUR

Disappointment flooded over me as I climbed on a bus headed back toward the youth hostel. I'd been so sure Ashlyn Meadowbrook and April Hill were one and the same. If April Hill really was dead, then my parents had been telling the truth about that at least. What was there left to do but go home?

Still, I certainly hadn't died as a toddler, so Ashlyn Meadowbrook was wrong about that. And if my birth mother was dead, I wanted to know the circumstances. My parents had never found April. So what did Ashlyn know that they didn't? If only we could have had more time to talk. Or if she'd been willing to at least tell me what she knew about the circumstances of those photos. If Ashlyn wouldn't be coming back to the gallery, was there some way I could find out where she lived and try again?

The bus driver, an older African-American man, checked my bus pass with a friendly nod. It occurred to me I did still have one clue to follow and that someone whose job involved driving around the city just might have information I needed.

Taking a seat in the front row across the aisle, I leaned forward and asked, "Excuse me, sir, but would you know anything about a wall of street art that's near a basketball court?"

The driver frowned thoughtfully. "There's a lot of street art in this city. Not so many basketball courts."

"Well, this one has a big, bright painting with the word 'created' in the middle and 'in Christ Jesus' underneath it."

"Ahh!" The driver's teeth flashed in his dark face. "Now that I do recognize. I learned that scripture as a kid, so I noticed it right off when it was painted—must be years ago now. That basketball court is part of the youth center at Morningside Neighborhood Church further north past the end of Central Park. I've been there myself. They have a lot of great community programs, including a youth basketball league, food pantry, and drug rehab program. The pastor is Reverend Yates. Been there forever—or decades at least."

"I'd like to visit the wall with the artwork. Could you tell me when we're at the nearest bus stop?"

"No trouble, young lady. I'll be stopping not far down the street from the church."

The bus pulled out and spent the next half-hour stopping and starting every few blocks before the driver waved a hand towards me. "Next stop is yours."

I thanked him as I exited. He gave me a wide smile. "You just take care of yourself. This isn't the best area for a young lady to be walking alone. You get in any trouble, you go look up Reverend Yates at the church."

He nodded up the street, where I could see the aged brick façade and tall steeple of a tired-looking old church. I didn't see a basketball court or the artwork I'd spotted so guessed those must be on the far side. As I exited with several other passengers, a tinge of unease filled me. The buildings weren't in good repair, and all the windows I saw had bars over them. Signs advertised a pawn shop, laundromat, check cashing business, and Hispanic bakery. Graffiti of the less artistic and more profane sort was splashed everywhere there was a flat surface.

A barefoot man in dirty jeans and shirt stood in the doorway of a corner convenience store, a cigarette dangling from his lips. He gave a wolf whistle as I hurried by and called something I was glad I didn't catch. Hearing him, three teen boys turned and stared at me. One muttered something in Spanish, and all three laughed.

My insides tightened as I picked up my pace, wondering again why I hadn't included Reese in my plans. I'd even gladly face my dad at this moment. I hesitated, considering calling either one, but forced myself to continue on.

I'd now reached the front façade of the church. Broad brick steps rose to the entrance. Once past the steps, I could see the basketball court I'd spotted during my previous bus ride. A high brick wall on the far side and back of the court along with the side of the church created a three-sided enclosure. A mesh fence topped with barbed wire separated the enclosure from the street.

A gate of steel tubing and mesh stood open, and a dozen teens were bouncing balls around the basketball court. As I approached, I could see the intricate details and vivid colors of street art covering both perimeter walls as well as the side of the church. The stylized letters of "Created" jumped out at me from the side wall, part of a much larger mural made up of people from different ethnicities doing activities like skateboarding, shooting hoops, reading, and flying a kite. Some images looked professional while others were little more than cartoon drawings.

I hurried toward the gate, pulling my camera from its case as I did so. The compass Reese had fastened to the strap of the bag caught my eye. As I slipped the camera strap over my head, his calm, deliberate voice rose to my mind. "For you. So if we're ever apart, you'll always be able to find your way back to me."

I pushed the memory away before homesickness could overcome me. Just then I heard quick, hard footsteps coming up behind me. I started to turn, but a violent, painful yank against my throat stopped me. Someone was trying to tear my camera from around my neck.

Fury boiled up inside me. The camera wasn't an expensive one, but it was a gift from my parents, and I wasn't about to let a stranger take it. Keeping one arm wrapped tightly around my camera, I twisted my body one way and then another. I felt out a sneaker-clad foot and stomped down as hard as I could. The grip loosened for a second. Pivoting, I brought my elbow backward. Moves my retired military father had drilled into me.

I heard a pained grunt. Then a fist punched me in the side of the head. The world spun around me, and I sank to my knees, wrapping my body around my camera to protect it from both damage and theft. A hard kick caught me in the ribs. Falling to my side, I rolled tighter into a ball. For the first time, I could see my attacker, an olive-skinned young man holding a knife. I kicked out, trying to sweep his legs from under him, but missed.

"Get away from her, man!" a voice shouted.

The three teen boys I'd seen earlier were racing toward me, no longer laughing. The attacker turned and ran. I pushed myself slowly to my feet, pain coursing through me. I was still holding my camera, but the compass Reese had given me was on the ground, its cover smashed.

Tears sprang to my eyes as I thought of Reese's words when he'd given me the compass and how angry he was at me for leaving him out. Now I needed him more than he could know. Growing up in small-town Indiana sure hadn't prepared me for New York City. I squeezed my eyes shut, my head throbbing from the punch to my face.

"Hey, you okay?"

I opened my eyes. The tallest of the three teens stood in front of me, a worried expression on his face. When I'd passed the trio, I'd felt intimidated and nervous. Had I judged them wrongly? They'd come to my rescue after all.

"Can you talk?" he asked. "Say something. You okay? I'm Raul by the way."

His name and accent confirmed some type of Hispanic heritage. I focused on him. "Yes. I'm Bailey. That guy tried to take my camera!"

"He's bad news. You pull out an expensive camera, you'd better be looking out for guys like him." It sounded funny that Raul called it an expensive camera when minutes earlier I'd been thinking I needed to upgrade. He gestured to the other two teens. "These two clowns are my brother Angelo and cousin Nico."

Angelo looked me up and down. "You look totally beat up. He do that?"

"No, I got in the way of a bicycle yesterday."

"Don't sound like you're doing too good," Raul said. "Why are you here in this neighborhood?"

"I wanted some photos of the street art over there in the church yard."

"A lady who volunteers at the center painted it. She had a camera too. Took our pictures," Angelo said.

"She said we'd be in some art show," Raul added.

Interest sparked in me. "This lady, was her name Ashlyn Meadowbrook? She has a photography exhibit called 'Faces of America'."

"Don't know. But she teaches art classes at the center." Nico waved an arm that encompassed the three walls of art. "That's her project. Me, I'm more into basketball and the martial arts classes. But I've got a sister who was in her class. She painted that corner over there."

Nico waved at a bit of mural that looked to be a youth spinning a basketball not unlike Nico with curly, dark hair and brown skin. "You take pictures too? Want us to model some martial arts poses?"

Raul scowled. "Don't push, Nico. She's about to fall over. Let's take her to the church. They'll patch her up."

The three teens walked with me through the gate and across the basketball court, weaving in between players, to a wooden door in the far wall. When Angelo pushed it open, I could see a short walkway leading to another building constructed of the same aged brick as the church. It ran perpendicular to the back of the church. To my left, another walkway connected the building to the church.

"The church offices and gym and classes and kitchen are all in here," Nico volunteered. "Reverend Yates will be around somewhere. He's used to pulling out the First Aid kit."

I hesitated at the door. "Are we allowed to walk in when there's no church services happening?"

Raul looked at me, amusement in his face. "You think churches are only for Sunday? Then you don't know this one. Reverend Yates practically lives here, and anyone's welcome any time the door's unlocked and the lights are on. Well, except maybe the punk who tried to take your camera."

Nico scoffed. "You know Reverend Yates would feed him a meal and send him away with a Bible. He says people can come to God just as they are. Whatever that means."

As the three teens led the way down a hall and into a small gym, an older African-American man looked up from a stack of plastic chairs he was wheeling across the polished wooden floor. Basketball hoops and portable soccer nets were pushed against walls at either end, and a dozen folding tables had already been set up in rows.

Raul led the way over to meet the man. He wore a clerical collar, but the rest of his dress was informal—a sports jacket over casual shirt and jeans. His buzz-cut tight curls were iron-gray, and he looked to be past retirement age. But his tall, straight carriage still looked strong and fit.

"Hey, Reverend, this is Bailey. She needs a bit of doctoring. She was taking some photos of the murals outside when some dude tried to get her camera. He punched her in the head, but she got in a couple of moves too."

I could feel the red of embarrassment burning my face. "It would have been a lot worse if these three hadn't stepped in."

Stepping forward to offer me a handshake, Reverend Yates gave the three teens an approving nod. "Well done, guys. How about you leave our guest with me and finish setting up these chairs. Bailey, why don't you follow me to the kitchen where we have more light and the First Aid kit."

The teen immediately began slinging chairs into place as we entered the kitchen through swinging double-doors on the right side of the gym. I was surprised to see it bustling with activity. Reverend Yates noticed my confusion. "We serve dinner here before the Wednesday evening service. A few church members come in early to start cooking."

Reaching under a counter, Reverend Yates pulled out a First Aid kit. As he drew me over to the light of a large window, he studied my face and let out a low whistle.

"It's not all from today." Yet again, I explained about the bike.

"Okay, let's get you cleaned up and bandaged." The reverend begin pulling items from the First Aid kit. "So what brings you here?"

"That wall mural with the scripture about being created in Christ Jesus." I winced as he used an antiseptic wipe to clean yesterday's wound. "I'm trying to find the person who painted it."

Reverend Yates covered the wound with gauze and taped it in place. "Oh, are you? Well, that part was painted by one of our volunteers who helps with some art classes for our youth center and drug rehab program. A pretty amazing artist, isn't she?"

"Yes, she sure is. Wait, you said the artist volunteers with a drug rehab program?"

I'd been concentrating on the basketball court I'd spotted on my first bus ride, so I'd forgotten the bus driver had mentioned a drug rehab program along with the other community outreaches. A thought niggled at my mind. That a famous uptown artist like Ashlyn Meadowbrook would volunteer in a place like this was surprising. But even famous people did charity work.

But a drug rehab program? My birth mother had been an addict according to my parents. Was that the connection between Ashlyn Meadowbrook and April Hill? Had April once been part of this church's rehab program, and that was how Ashlyn ended up doing her photo shoots as some kind of charity? The bus driver had said Reverend Yates had been here for decades. Maybe Reverend Yates knew April Hill.

But, no, the photos had been taken when I was a baby and my parents were still in April Hill's life. So what connection did Ashlyn Meadowbrook have to both my birth mother and this church that she volunteered here? That at least Reverend Yates might be able to help me with.

The reverend was still speaking as he packed away the First Aid supplies. "Yes, our rehab program meets several times during the week for group discussion, counseling, and whatever help they need. This church is a safe place for many different groups of people. We greatly appreciate our volunteers who make our programs possible, many of whom were once in similar situations and so are happy to give back now that God has turned their own lives around."

His words caught my attention. Was past drug addiction the connection between Ashlyn and April? Was that why Ashlyn seemed so freaked at the mention of Martin Beck? Had he dragged her down as he'd once done April? Was that why she'd called him dangerous? Maybe they'd even known each other before Martin came along. After all, hadn't Dad said his sister—April's mom—had also been a drug addict?

All the mental questions were making my head ache even worse. I spoke aloud. "Was the person who painted the wall art part of your rehab program before she became a volunteer here at your church? Was the rehab program how she found the faith to create the artwork about being God's creation?"

Oh, and by the way, is your volunteer's name Ashlyn Meadowbrook?

"Now, young lady, I'm sure you can appreciate we can't give out personal information on our volunteers or whether or not they were in our programs." The reverend's smile took some of the sting from his rebuke. "But you're welcome to photograph the artwork. And join us for this evening's meal and church service if you like."

Deflated, I shook my head. "I don't think so. I'm feeling a bit beat up."

"I can see that." Reverend Yates's black eyes twinkled down at me. He paused and gave me a long look that seemed to see into my soul before adding, "But if you need any kind of help or merely want to talk, I'm here. I'll be in the sanctuary for the next hour or so getting ready for tonight. But don't hesitate to interrupt me."

I thanked him and wandered outside. Raul, Angelo, and Nico were out on the basketball court shooting hoops. I rubbed the back of my neck where a headache was starting as I headed over to the wall mural. I wasn't sure what to do next. If only Ashlyn been willing to talk to me. Or Reverend Yates had been more forthcoming. I was left with bits and pieces of a story that didn't add up and not a single remaining lead.

Maybe the church has files with contact data. Didn't volunteers have to do a background check? But breaking into the church office was beyond what even my imagination could contemplate.

I walked around aimlessly, taking photos of the street art and several action shots of the basketball game now in progress. If nothing else, I wanted to document my trip in photos. This might be my only adventure for the foreseeable future since I'd probably be grounded the rest of the summer once my parents found out what I'd done.

I was kneeling, my camera zoomed in on Raul, who was going for a layup, when a chill went through me. Still kneeling, I zoomed out and adjusted the camera slightly. I hadn't been mistaken. Caught in the crosshairs of my lens, Martin stood outside the mesh fence and across the street, his narrowed gaze glued on the street art mural above my head.

CHAPTER TWENTY-FIVE

I stayed crouched, camera raised to my eye in such a way I could only hope disguised my identity. I didn't dare make a movement that might drag Martin's attention away from the mural. An eternity later—or maybe mere seconds—he turned away and headed across the street in the direction of the church entrance.

The moment he was out of sight, I straightened up and hurried to the mesh fence. The street in front of the church was empty. Martin must have gone inside. I didn't try following him but hurried to the wooden door in the wall leading to the church annex. As with the gallery, I had to assume he'd followed the same clues I'd found online, including the street art on Ashlyn's website.

Which meant he'd probably also seek out information at the church as I'd done. And somehow I couldn't see Martin politely accepting Reverend Yates's reticence as I'd had to do. I quickened my pace, suddenly worried for the kindly old reverend.

I'd just stepped into the annex hallway when my phone rang. Without looking at the Caller ID, I hurriedly pulled it from my pocket and muted it. If it was one of my parents, they'd assume I didn't have access to my phone. Draya would be on her flight. Angry or not, Reese might be calling, if only to chew me out for having kept him in the dark. But that was a distraction I couldn't afford right now.

I hurried down the hall. A low buzz of voices was coming from the gym where volunteers were setting up for supper. But Reverend Yates had said he'd be in the sanctuary, so Martin had likely already intercepted him. Reaching the next walkway, I quietly eased the door open. I immediately heard a rumble of male voices, one calm, the other sounding angry.

I slipped through the opening, careful to make no noise. The door opened onto the left side of a low platform with a pump organ filling the rest of the space. The sanctuary was small and as dated as the exterior with long wooden benches, high stained-glass windows, an ornate altar, and a podium centered at the front of the platform.

I could now hear the conversation clearly enough to be sure the speakers were Martin and Reverend Yates. The last thing I wanted was for Martin to catch me here, so I slid behind theater drapes pulled back to the rear of the platform. The podium blocked my view of the pastor, but I could see Martin leaning forward aggressively.

"I know she painted the mural on the wall out there," he said angrily. "Where is she?"

"I can't give information on our congregants or volunteers without their consent," Reverend Yates said pleasantly but firmly. "No matter how many ways you phrase the question. As I've said, all I can do is pass on your request through the proper channels and see if the volunteer in question is interested in responding."

"So you do have her contact information. Why don't we take a walk together back to your office, and we can give her a call together."

If I couldn't see Reverend Yate beyond the podium, I saw Martin lunge forward and heard a grunt of pain. To be this bold, Martin must not realize there were other people in the building. I slid silently from behind the curtains and back out the still cracked-open door. If I could get to the gym, I could call out for help.

But I'd only taken one long stride when I collided with Raul. Angelo and Nico were right behind him, Nico still holding a basketball under one arm.

Raul put his hand out to steady me. "What's happened now?"

"There's a guy in there threatening your pastor," I gasped out. "A really bad guy. We need to get help."

Raul's eyebrows shot up. "Does trouble follow you everywhere, Señorita Bailey? Don't worry about Reverend Yates. He can take care of himself. He's probably counseling the guy."

"No, you don't understand!" I said desperately. "I know who this guy is. He's into drug-dealing and has been in jail. He's dangerous. We've got to get help!"

Their expressions immediately changed, all three teens now looking rather dangerous themselves.

"We'll take care of him," Raul said grimly. "No one threatens our reverend and gets away with it."

Raul pushed into the church sanctuary, followed by Nico and Angelo. Through the open door, I could see Martin pushing Reverend Yates ahead of him in our direction, one hand tightly gripping the elderly pastor's sports jacket. I stayed back out of sight as the three teens blocked the way.

"You need to leave," Raul announced.

"Now," Angelo added.

Martin didn't release his grip on Reverend Yates but balled his free fist. "Get lost, punks. The last thing you want is to get in a fight with me. This is between me and the reverend, and I'm not leaving until I get the information I need."

Raul took a long step forward. "It doesn't look like the reverend wants to give you information."

Nico stepped up beside him. "And we'd love to get in a fight with you, right, guys? Three against one is better odds than I've ever had."

Angelo pulled out a cell phone. "Nah, he's not worth another stint in juvie. Let's just call 911 for a change."

Martin looked from one teen to the other, seeming to recognize for the first time that maybe these weren't three clueless, peaceable church youth but street fighters with some experience of violence under their own belts. I stood frozen, hoping Martin wasn't about to pull out a gun or other weapon.

Instead, he released the reverend's jacket and raised his hands, palms out. "Hey, I'm not trying to cause trouble here. Just looking for some answers."

He glared at Reverend Yates, who simply stood there quietly. "And don't think this is the end of this. If I don't find April, I'll be back, count on it!"

Martin turned and angrily stormed down the aisle toward the front door, the three teens following. Raul called over his shoulder, "We'll be back, Reverend, just as soon as we make sure this guy finds his way off church property."

I stayed out of sight behind the theater curtain as the teens followed Martin out the front door. My phone began vibrating again, and I put my hand over it, willing it to stop. Thankfully, I'd silenced the ring tone. But even the quiet buzz was enough to draw Reverend Yate's attention.

He walked over and tugged the theater curtain away. "Bailey. Why am I not surprised to find you part of this? Do you have something you'd like to tell me?"

I couldn't pretend I didn't know what he meant. Not with Martin asking the same questions I had. And the astute kindness in his dark eyes made me swallow hard. I suddenly felt about two years old and wishing desperately this was my dad standing there and I could throw myself into his arms and burst into tears.

"Yes, yes, I think I do," I admitted. "But—could we go somewhere private where we won't be interrupted?"

"Of course. Come with me. We can talk in my office. " The elderly reverend led the way back into the annex, then turned left down the hall the opposite direction from the gym. He opened a door and ushered me inside. In front of a large desk were several comfortable armchairs. He waved me to one, then sat down across from me.

"Okay, Bailey, you want to tell me what this is all about? Who is this man, and why are you both so intent on contacting the person who painted the mural out there?"

I hesitated, not sure where to start. But encouraged by his kindly gaze, I launched into my story, starting with finding my baby photos, then the search that had led me to this church.

"Two of my friends helped me figure out some of the truth. I know April Hill is my birth mom, and the man who just left says he's my birth father. So the people I grew up believing were my parents are really my uncle and aunt. And I know Ashlyn Meadowbrook took the pictures of me. So if she isn't April Hill herself, she has to know something about her. She told me April Hill was dead, but then she thought I was dead too. So I have to contact her to find out what else she knows."

Reverend Yates looked at me thoughtfully. "You know I can't give you that information. I can only offer what I told Martin—to contact the volunteer in question and see if she'd be willing to speak with you."

"Please, that would be a start," I pleaded. "It's not just about me. I'm worried she could be in danger. Especially if Martin tracked her here like I did. I don't know why he's so determined to find her, but I don't think it's anything good because Ashlyn seemed really panicked to find out he was in New York and looking for April."

Reverend Yates rubbed his chin. "I don't think there's any point now of holding back that the volunteer in question is indeed Ashlyn Meadowbrook. I got to know her a good decade back when she was new in this city. She's done a lot of good work in our community programs. She's never talked much about her past, but she did tell me she'd done an exhibit of baby pictures in memory of a child. Now that I've met Martin, I can see he's dangerous. And I believe you're telling the truth as far as you know it about being the baby in those pictures. I'll call her right now."

I waited with tense eagerness as he pulled out a cell-phone and tapped on an entry in his contact list. But my shoulders slumped when he listened briefly, then said, "Ashlyn, Reverend Yates here. I need to talk to you as soon as possible. Could you call me as soon as you receive this message?"

Ringing off, the reverend turned to me. "Looks like we have another wait ahead. In the meantime, may I ask a question of my own? I noticed when you asked about Ashlyn's mural that you recognized the words 'created' and 'in Christ Jesus' as being from Scripture. Do you know the meaning of the words?"

I hesitated, not used to talking about spiritual things with a preacher. "My friend Reese said it means God created us to do good things for God and others. He said my photography, his athletic skills, and our friend Draya's computer skills are all from God."

The reverend nodded. "What your friend said is correct. God had a plan for you before you were born. He gave you the abilities you need to carry it out. More than that, he created you as a unique, one-of-a-kind person. So while you're searching for your true identity, I pray you will let that search lead you to God. He alone gives you true purpose and identity."

"How?" I asked. "Everything I thought true about myself is a lie."

Reverend Yates rubbed his chin again. "I don't have the answer, but from your story, it sounds like your parents, even if not your birth father and mother, love you very much. So maybe you can at least have faith that whatever led to you living with them and even keeping the truth from you was out of a desire to protect you. And even if you can't see it yet, you can trust God had a plan even in that."

He got to his feet. "Now, I believe I'm smelling spaghetti or perhaps lasagna. Why don't you go get some dinner while I keep trying to get a hold of Ashlyn. Oh, and give me your number so I can text you the moment I hear something."

He ripped a Post-It off a pad on his desk and handed it to me along with a pen. I scribbled my number and handed it back. "Thank you so much. I can't say how much I appreciate this— all of it."

I followed him to the door, but before I could step into the hall, I heard loud, boisterous voices. Raul, Nico, and Angelo burst through the door leading into the sanctuary and headed our direction.

"Mission accomplished," Raul announced. "He's on a bus headed downtown."

"Well done. Let's hope he doesn't come back any time soon," Reverend Yates said. "I'll alert the church leaders to keep an eye out and be ready to call the police if he shows up again tonight. Meanwhile, why don't you three take Bailey to get some dinner."

He turned to me. "I'll let you know when I have any further news on that phone call."

His statement drew curious glances from the three teens. But they didn't ask any further questions until we were seated at a table, plates loaded with lasagna and bread. Then Raul leaned forward.

"So what's up with you, girl? You come to New York and get beat up at least twice. Then this guy threatens the reverend, and you clearly know something about him. And now the reverend's making calls for you? Spill it!"

"It's complicated." The last thing I wanted was to tell my entire story again. "The short version is I came to New York in search of my birth mom. That guy is trying to find her too. And Reverend Yates is trying to help me track down someone who might have some information."

I met three skeptical stares, but the three teens didn't push further. We finished our meal. Then Raul spoke up. "Okay, guys, it's our evening to help with dinner cleanup. Bailey, you're welcome to stick around for our youth meeting. It will be right here in the gym once we get the tables and chairs put away."

I grimaced. Exhaustion was catching up to me, and all I needed was to spend the evening explaining myself over and over to more strangers. "I appreciate the invite, but I'm waiting around to hear back from Reverend Yates on a phone call. Then I'm headed out."

Pushing myself to my feet, I gathered up my dirty dishes, then turned back to the three teens. "I do want to say thanks again. You've been great. And—keep an eye on the reverend. I . . . well, I'd hate to see him in trouble again on my account."

Their expressions immediately went from smiling to stern. Raul spoke up firmly. "You don't need to worry about that. We're all here because Reverend Yates cared enough to pull us off the streets before it was too late for us. Believe me, no one is going to mess with our reverend if we have anything to say about it!"

Looking from one hard face to the other, I suddenly had no difficulty believing it.

CHAPTER TWENTY-SIX

Slipping back into the church sanctuary, I headed down the aisle and outside to the street. Even though the teens had said they'd put Martin on a bus, I found myself searching for him in all directions. Reassured, I walked aimlessly down the street several blocks and back again, hoping for the ding of an incoming text.

But none came, so I made my way back to the sanctuary. The evening services had clearly started as there was a group of maybe twenty adults at the front of the sanctuary, and Reverend Yates was addressing them, gesturing with his hands as he made key points. I found a pew at the very back and settled in, figuring I'd at least wait until the service was over before giving up on hearing back from Ashlyn tonight.

Apprehension dancing in me, I played out different scenarios in my mind. Would Ashlyn know anything about my birth mother? She'd said April Hill was dead, but could I trust her word? And why was she so scared of Martin Beck? Had she once been involved in his drug-dealing? Was I crazy to be still sitting here instead of calling my parents? Or at least Reese?

The meeting seemed to last forever, but it was really only an hour or so before people began exiting the church. Reverend Yates was the last to leave the front of the sanctuary. I saw him lift his cell-phone to his ear and speak for several minutes before heading my way down the aisle. He lowered himself onto the pew beside me.

"I'm glad to find you still here as I spoke to Ashlyn. I told her about you and the earlier incident with Martin." He paused and studied me. I remained silent, waiting to hear more. He let out a sigh. "I have to say she remains reluctant to have me give you her contact information."

My heart plummeted. "She still thinks I'm lying?"

"She's concerned you're part of whatever plan this Martin has in trying to track her down. But there is good news. She refused to let me give you her phone number or address. But she's agreed to meet with you here at the church so long as I'm present as well."

Reverend Yates smiled kindly at me. "For what it's worth, I believe you, including that you are the child in those photos, and I told her so. I think once you're face to face, she will see the truth. It had to have been a shock for her to be told you really are alive."

He was interrupted as Raul, Nico, and Angelo burst into the sanctuary and down the aisle.

"Everything good here?" Raul asked. "No sign of that creep?"

"We're fine. I'm simply talking with Bailey."

"Want us to hang around till you're done?" Nico offered. "Everyone else is out."

"No. Thank you for the kind offer, but we don't need any bodyguards," Reverend Yates responded with a grin. "I appreciate all the help you've been, but I happen to know you three all work in the morning. You need your beauty sleep."

All three teens made noises of disgust, but they headed for the door. At the rear, Raul paused. "Lock up once we're out, okay, Reverend?"

Reverend Yates waved a shooing hand. "I did manage to survive before you three came along. Go home and get some sleep!"

As they left, he turned to me. "They aren't wrong. I'll lock up as soon as Ashlyn shows. Then we can head to my office."

I was vibrating on the edge of my pew by the time the front door of the sanctuary opened. Ashlyn Meadowbrook stepped inside. Reverend Yates rose to his feet and walked over to greet her, then stepped past to lock the door. I could hardly breathe as Ashlyn walked over to me.

"Okay, I do see it," Reverend Yates said quietly behind her.

We both looked at him. He shook his head from side to side. "I still remember the girl who walked into this church a good ten years ago grieving her baby daughter. Now that your hair is grown out and its original color, you sure could be sisters."

He turned to Ashlyn. "Do you want to tell her the name you gave me then, or should I?"

I couldn't breathe as Ashlyn stared at me somberly, studying my face as if under a microscope. Then she spoke almost inaudibly. "I haven't heard that name in a decade."

I stared, not sure what to make of this turn of events. "You *are* April Hill? My birth mother? Then why did you tell me April Hill is dead?"

She gave me another long look before answering. "She is dead, at least to me. That person is gone, thankfully. But, yes, once upon a time I was April Hill. And once upon a time I had a daughter. But she's dead. So whatever story you've fed Reverend Yates, it can't be true. I only came here to find out what trouble you and Martin are dragging Reverend Yates and this church into."

"I'm telling the truth!" I cried out. "And I can prove it."

"Ladies, why don't we adjourn to my office," Reverend Yates interrupted firmly. "I think an honest talk between the two of you will get all this straightened out.

I followed silently on Ashlyn's heels as Reverend Yates led the way down the aisle and through the hall to his office. I sank into the chair I'd occupied before as Ashlyn sat reluctantly across from me. Reverend Yates remained standing.

"Bailey, show Ashlyn the photos you showed me. I'm going to do a turn around the kitchen and make sure everything's cleaned and put away. I'll be back in a bit."

He strode from the office but left the door open. There was an awkward silence as Ashlyn and I eyed each other. Then she asked abruptly, "What pictures?"

I pulled out my cell-phone and opened my photo album to the pictures I'd used in my family tree project. As I did so, I noticed I now had six missed calls. No caller could be more important than this, so I ignored them, pulling up that earliest portrait when I was somewhere around a year old. Anxiety and hope churned in my stomach as I handed it to Ashlyn. This was it. Either she'd recognize this photo, or I'd been lied to still again.

For a long moment, Ashlyn didn't make a sound. I sat frozen as she scrolled through the other photos on my phone, stopping when she reached the end. She raised her head, and I saw tears were streaming down her face.

"This is you?" she whispered, scrolling back to a recent

photo of me with my parents. She tapped the screen. "You were with my brother Tim and his wife Patty all this time?"

"Then you believe me? That I'm your daughter?"

She nodded, running a hand through her hair. "Your parents! I can't believe that's where you've been all these years. That you really are my Summer. Martin told me you were dead. It didn't even occur to me he could be lying."

I stared at her. "What do you mean? Why would you believe something like that without proof?"

She tightened her lips and looked away. I reached out a hand, pleading, "Please, it's too late for any more secrets. I have to know the truth, whatever it is. Just tell me."

She let out her breath and settled back into the chair before she began speaking, her voice low and her eyes somewhere on the wall above my head.

"I don't know what my brother and his wife told you about me. I'm sure it was all true as they aren't the sort to lie and I was a mess back then. I'd been in and out of the drug scene since my early teens till my mom overdosed. Then I got stuck with a brother I didn't even know and old enough to be my dad. They tried to be nice, I know now. I just thought they were ridiculously strict. Then I met Martin and ran off with him."

A look of deep regret crossed her face. "I want you to know I really did try to kick my drug habit while I was pregnant and even afterwards. I moved back in with my brother. That's when I took all those pictures. But they wanted me to be the good, responsible mom. I was only nineteen. I loved my baby, but I still wanted to have fun, and Martin promised me that. He said we'd be a family. But as soon as I moved back with you, he got me started on drugs again. I think he wanted me hooked so I wouldn't say anything about his drug operation."

I gasped. "Then he really was a drug dealer?"

"Big time. I didn't have anything to do with his operation. He told me I was too flaky to trust. And pretty soon he was tired of having a crying baby around. He told me to send you back to my brother. When I refused, well—a couple weeks later I woke up one morning and you were gone. He told me I'd accidentally killed you in a blackout."

Shock ran through me. "He told you you'd killed me? That's awful! And you believed him?"

She shrugged. "I had no reason not to. I'd had plenty of blackouts while using in the past, even crashed a car once while I was high and almost died. He told me he'd buried her—I mean, you—to keep me from going to prison."

Her face twisted with grief. "And to think I was actually grateful to him!"

"So how did I end up with my aunt and uncle? Didn't you bother even checking to find out if that's where Martin took me?" I shook my head hard, feeling more confused than ever. Questions rolled from my lips.

"And what happened to you? My parents said they looked for you. That you were dead. But—they also changed their names and mine. I didn't know my dad's last name was Hill until I found pictures he'd hidden away. Did they kidnap me? Why would they if Martin gave me to them? Were they afraid you'd take me back? And where have you been all these years? How did you end up Ashlyn Meadowbrook in New York City instead of April Hill in Chicago?"

Ashlyn straightened up and banished the tears from her face with the back of one hand. "I don't know all those answers. But I can tell you where I've been. I guess Martin figured getting rid of you would mean I'd settle back to being the party girl he fell in love with. But I was so devasted at the thought I'd killed my own daughter I left him that same night. I hitched a ride east, eventually found myself in New York City. I should be dead as far down as I lost myself in the drug scene. The only thing I didn't do was deliberately kill myself, but I did my best to let the drugs do it."

Her face softened, and she turned her head to look straight at me. "Then one evening, I walked in the doors of this church. I only did so because I hadn't eaten in days and could smell food cooking. I was reasonably sober because I hadn't had money for a fix in days either. I sat in the back pew, right where you were when I walked in, not wanting to go any further but too weak to walk back out. That's where Reverend Yates found me."

She gave a twisted smile. I didn't need any explanation. I'd had my own encounter with the tough, unyielding kindness of Reverend Yates.

"It took a while," Ashlyn went on. "But that was basically the end of April Hill and the beginning of a new identity. He got me into their rehab program. Found a church member willing to give a guest bedroom to a recovering junkie. Later on helped me get my first job with a photography studio. A new name was the cherry on top of being a brand-new person. Or at least that's what I felt like."

"Created in Christ Jesus," I murmured.

"That's right. Reverend Yates said you tracked me here by

my artwork. If I'd dreamed anyone was still looking for me, I'd have painted it over. But that verse meant a lot to me, though it took a while for me to really believe God valued me and created me with a purpose like Reverend Yates kept telling me."

Ashlyn took in a deep breath. "The hardest part was forgiving myself for killing you. Once I was—well, fairly sane again and had earned enough money for a bus ticket, I went back to Chicago to see if Martin was still at the house we shared. I had some crazy idea of turning myself in and confessing what had happened. But he was gone, and the house was closed up. So I walked the whole ten miles to Tim's old house. But he was gone too. I asked the neighbors, but no one had any idea where he'd gone or why. I even did an internet search, figuring since he'd been in the military, he might be in some database. But it was like he'd dropped off the planet as completely as I had."

She looked past me as though reliving those days. "I began to wonder if I was going crazy. If I'd imagined I had a daughter or a brother or the time of peace and family I'd had with him. But I knew I wasn't crazy because I still had Summer's pictures to prove she was real."

Ashlyn brought her gaze back to my face. "So where did Tim take you all those years ago?"

"Actually, I've spent my entire life as far as I've known it in smalltown Indiana. Dad owns a mechanic shop, and Mom helps him in the business. I couldn't figure out why there were no pictures of me when I was a baby or why they were so paranoid about having any presence on the internet. I really did begin to think maybe they were in the witness protection program or something like that. Then I found old pictures of myself I'd never known about. And there was a picture of Dad in a uniform that had a different last name on it, so my friend Draya arranged a DNA test for me. It was a big shock to find out my parents weren't my birth parents."

I hunched my shoulders. "That's the part I still don't understand. Why they would have run with me. And lied about it. It goes against everything they ever taught me about right and wrong."

"Actually, that part I understand completely," Ashlyn said softly. As I gave her a sharp look, she met my eyes squarely. "I want to be angry with my brother for letting me think you were dead all these years. But I know Martin, and I know Tim. If he left everything behind and changed his name in order to raise you as his child, he must have believed he was rescuing you from Martin. That Martin would come after you if he knew where you were. And he'd be right. Martin may not have wanted you himself, but he'd never have let Tim and Patty have you."

Ashlyn made a weary gesture. "Believe me, Martin doesn't let go of anything he owns. He'd rather destroy it than let someone else have it. That's why I had to get out of there once he told me you were dead. I knew he'd never let me go freely. And if Tim told you I was dead, maybe Martin told him the same kind of lie he told me."

She stood up and walked over to me. I rose from my seat. Our faces were only inches apart. I could see in her features the same bone structure, blue eyes, even dimple we both shared with my dad. Her expression melted, and I think mine did too because she suddenly wrapped her arms tight around me. My arms rose to her back. I could feel my tears on her cheeks. Or maybe hers on mine.

"I don't care about any of that," she said into my hair. "What matters is you're alive. Of all the miracles God's done in my life, this is not one I ever expected. Despite everything I did wrong, God is giving me a second chance with you. Whatever else there is to know, we'll learn soon enough."

The crash of the office door against the wall made us both jump. I spun around, startled but not wary since Reverend Yates was the only other person in the building.

Or should have been. It was indeed Reverend Yates who'd knocked the door into the wall. But only because he'd been pushed. Standing behind him, gun in hand and hatred lining his face, was Martin Beck.

CHAPTER TWENTY-SEVEN

My mouth went dry, my stomach knotting, as Martin shoved Reverend Yates into the office. The reverend's arms were zip-tied behind him, and a gag bit deeply into his mouth, but his gaze was both apologetic and composed. He held my gaze as though trying to radiate comfort, and he even succeeded to some extent.

Beside me, my birth mom slid trembling fingers into mine. I squeezed her hand. Martin's mouth twisted into a contemptuous sneer as he caught the gesture. "So I guess you've introduced yourself to our daughter, April. I'm sorry to have missed the big reunion."

Ashlyn straightened to her full slim height. "You told me she was dead! That I'd killed my own baby. All these years I believed that. How could you?"

"How could I? How can you ask that? You were a junkie! The only reason you didn't kill her one way or another is because you didn't have time. You let her fall down the stairs and break her arm while you were shooting up. Remember that? What kind of a mother does that? She was better off without you."

"You mean, you were better off without her! You were the one who didn't want her around the house, needing fed, making noise. As to the drugs, you were the one who convinced me I needed them to realize my full artistic ability. And got me back on them after Summer and I came back to you."

She broke off and waved her free hand. "None of that matters. What matters is what you did with Summer. She was gone. You told me she was dead. Where was she?"

He shrugged. "Not far. I had someone watching her at the warehouse. She'd have been fine. Unlike you, I'd never hurt my own daughter. I had a nice couple ready to pay big money for her no questions asked. Until your brother interfered. Do I have a score to settle with him! And not just for hauling off a brat who wouldn't stop screaming from the moment her mother walked out!"

Martin shifted his sneer to me. "Believe me, since the day I walked out of prison, I've had two thoughts on my mind. One, to find April and get what's mine back. And to pay back the person who stuck me behind bars. So once I get what's mine, you're going to tell me where to find Sergeant Timothy Hill, or whatever he's calling himself these days. Although I know he has to be in that dinky town you call home. I didn't have time to stick around and find him after your school friend gave me the first big clue on where to find April."

He turned his gaze back to Ashlyn. "But first, where is it, April?"

"Where is what?"

I glanced at my birth mom. She looked as confused as she sounded.

Martin waved the gun in a way Dad had taught me never to do. "Don't act so innocent, April! My backup stash. Twenty kilos of it. Five million street value. I didn't put in twelve years behind bars waiting to get out and start over to let you walk off with it."

I gasped. "Five million! You mean, drugs? So that's why you

were looking for us? Not to find your family but your drug stash?"

His chill gaze touched my face. "Family? There isn't a person on this earth I wouldn't trade five million for, so you might want to remember that."

Martin took a step forward. "What did you do with the cocaine that was in our house, April? And a quarter-million cash? Give it to your brother? Is that why he left?"

Ashlyn shook her head hard. "I don't know what you're talking about, Martin. You were still in that house when I left. It was years before I ever went back, and by then you were gone and the house all shut up. If you still had drugs there, why would you think I'd have taken them instead of your crew. They knew more about your drug operation than I ever did. I didn't even know you were in prison."

"No one knew where I kept my backup stash. And you were the only other person in the house day in and out who might have found it. Unless you're suggesting the kid did it!"

Ashlyn shook her head sadly. "Do you think I wouldn't tell you if I knew? Or that I'd have kept drugs around all this time? You can ask Reverend Yates if I had a penny when I met him. Or now other than my art sales. Look over my accounts if you want. If I had your drugs, believe me I'd have turned them over to the police. God freed me from that world ten years ago, and I've never looked back. Now I'm free to be who God created me to be."

"Who God created you to be?" Martin let out a raucous laugh. "Are you telling me you of all people bought into the God thing? Now that is funny!"

He laughed again with a lack of humor that sent a chill through me. I moved closer to Ashlyn until our shoulders were touching. She gripped my hand tighter as she raised her chin in a gesture I'd seen on my own face in the mirror.

"Yes, I bought into the God thing, and I want nothing more to do with you or your lifestyle. I don't have your drugs or your money, so why don't you do one good thing for your daughter and let us go. Find the guys who drove for you. Who sold your stuff on the streets. If you went to prison, they probably cleaned you out. Or maybe they ratted you out to the DEA or some other law enforcement who found your stash."

I listened to the two strangers I now knew to be my birth parents with confusion. The world they were discussing was a far cry from the life I'd grown up with. Suddenly, a deep longing for my parents filled me. My real parents. Ashlyn might be my birth mom and this creep my birth father. But my real parents were miles away in Indiana, not realizing I was in any kind of trouble.

I looked over at Reverend Yates, who stood quietly to one side, his gaze focused on the waving gun in Martin's hand. The reverend suddenly looked up at me and gave the tiniest fraction of a nod. What did he mean? That he had a plan? To trust that God had a plan?

I squeezed my eyes shut, pleading silently, *Please, God, if you have a plan here, this would be a good time to use it!*

"Why would you say that about a raid? Are you the one who tipped off the cops when all this time I thought it was your brother?" I opened my eyes in time to see Martin lash out and catch Ashlyn across the face with his gun. She fell back, her grip torn from mine. Blood spurted from a gash on her cheekbone.

"Stop!" I fell to my knees beside Ashlyn. Grabbing at the hem of my T-shirt to staunch the blood, I glared up at Martin. "How could you do that? I'm so glad my dad took me away from you!"

Martin raised his gun threateningly, and I thought he was going to hit me too. Reverend Yates moved forward, and Martin spun around, leveling the gun at him. The reverend froze mid-step.

Reaching into his pocket, Martin pulled out several zip-ties. With the same hand, he yanked me to my feet, the zip-ties in his hand biting into my skin. "You and April are coming with me. Put one of these on your mom, then I'll deal with you."

He spun toward Reverend Yates. "You are too big and old to lug along and too high-profile to kill. Last thing I need is another manhunt. There has to be some place on this property I can stash you where you won't be found for a day or two since your schedule out there says no services till Sunday."

He swung back around and dropped a zip-tie in front of where I was kneeling. "Now, Summer, get that zip-tie on your mom, then stand and put your hands behind you."

My heart was racing so fast I felt it would burst from my chest. My breath came in shallow gasps. Ashlyn leaned forward close enough to grab my hand in bloody fingers. "It's okay, Summer. God has our back. I really believe the message I painted on that wall. God created us to do good things for him. I believe he still has more for us to do, and he will bring us through this."

"Very touching!" Martin sneered. "Here, give me that!"

Leaning forward, he snatched up the zip-tie he'd dropped,

slid the gun into his waistband, then moved behind Ashlyn and bound her hands together so tightly it caused her to cry out. But before he could move to bind my own wrists, a thud of heavy footsteps rushed down the hall outside the office.

Reverend Yates had only time to move out of the way before a pair of large, fast-moving male bodies burst into the office. Martin grabbed the gun from his waistband. But before he could raise it, the same male bodies tackled him simultaneously, sending the gun spinning across the carpet and under a chair.

I'd prayed for God to do something. I'd even had in mind a possible plan. That plan had included the only three people I knew in New York City God might possibly bring to our rescue. The three teens who'd saved the day twice already in the last few hours.

But it wasn't Raul, Nico, or Angelo who rolled to a sitting position on Martin's midriff and said in a hard voice, "Hand me those zip-ties and let's see how he likes being tied up."

Or who slid in one smooth move under the chair, scooped up Martin's gun, and cocked it straight down at Martin's stunned face.

"Dad! Reese!" I shrieked. "Where did you come from?"

And then I did what I'd resisted doing for days. Weeks. I burst into tears and rushed into my dad's arms.

CHAPTER TWENTY EIGHT

"Hey, need any more help here?" a familiar voice with a slight Hispanic accent called out.

I pulled myself from my dad's arms to look toward the open doorway. Raul stepped through, Angelo and Nico at his heels. He looked from Martin, now hogtied on his side, arms behind his back, and what looked like Reese's belt connecting his wrists with his zip-tied ankles, to the gun in Dad's hand.

"Looks like you got things handled, Mr.—?"

"Collins," Dad said automatically. "Tim Collins."

Then his glance moved past me to Ashlyn. "April!"

His voice shook like—well, like he'd seen something very precious he'd thought he'd lost. And suddenly my birth mom was pushing past me into his arms as I'd done, their whispered words not reaching anyone but each other.

Sirens sounded in the distance as Reese stood up and pulled me into a tight hug. Behind him, Martin was letting loose a steady stream of profanity the approaching sirens thankfully drowned out.

I pulled back from Reese, looked from him to the three teens in the doorway. "Thanks for saving the day, guys. But would someone tell me how you all managed to show up in the nick of time?"

I looked up at Reese, then over at my dad, who was still speaking in a low voice to Ashlyn as he wiped at her bloody face.

Dad looked up at me, and I repeated the question. "You especially. Where did you come from?"

"We let them in," Raul said.

"I hope we did right!" Nico added anxiously. "They said you were family. That they were afraid you were in trouble."

"You weren't answering your phone," Reese's deep voice cut in. "You always answer your phone."

"And we knew you had it," Angelo broke in. "And you'd stayed behind with Reverend Yates. So we thought the creep might have come back."

Their voices were suddenly a jumble of talking over each other so that my head began to swim. "Reverend Yates told us to leave, but we didn't trust that creep not to come back . . . We posted a guard . . . Never saw that guy but caught these two sneaking around outside . . . Yeah, figured they must be with him . . . The old guy said he was your dad, and he looks like you . . . your boyfriend showed us pictures of you two at school, so we figured they weren't lying . . . Everything was locked, so we couldn't get in . . . The reverend wasn't answering his phone either, but his car was still here . . . Your dad said your phone tracker showed you were here. Next thing we know, he busted a kitchen window . . . And, well, by time we got here, it was over."

My boyfriend? It probably meant something that calling Reese my boyfriend was the one thing that jumped out of the flood of words. But a shrill whistle suddenly brought complete silence. Even Martin on the floor shut up.

Someone had cut loose Reverend Yates's zip-tied wrists and gag. He stepped forward into the middle of the chaos. "Okay, if we could get some peace and quiet around here, maybe someone—"

He gave the three teens a stern look. "—as in one at a time, can explain exactly what happened here."

One arm still around Ashlyn, Dad stretched out a hand and shook the reverend's heartily. "I'm Tim Collins. Actually, Tim Hill. You've met my daughter Bailey. And my sister April. And it seems I owe you a lot of thanks for being here for both my girls."

He might have said more, but just then there was a thunderous crash we found out later was the police using a battering ram on the sanctuary doors. A moment later, a dozen police officers were pouring through the building, shouting, "Clear! Clear!"

It was an hour or more before I had a chance to talk to my dad and Reese again or Ashlyn—no, April—either. Two officers quickly traded out zip-ties for handcuffs and led Martin away. The rest of us were taken to different areas of the church to give our statements.

I'd wanted to be there when Dad and Reese told their story of how they'd managed to rush in exactly when needed most. I could give credit this was some miracle from God as Reverend Yates had suggested. But since I didn't figure they'd been bodily transported like some Star Trek episode, I'd have liked to know how they did end up crashing through a window of Morningside Neighborhood Church.

But finally the police and Martin were both gone, all but a single squad car keeping watch over the busted-in front doors. Raul, Angelo, and Nico made their farewells with evident reluctance. "You ever come back to New York City, don't be strangers now. And you need help taking down any more perps, give us a call."

"We'll do that." Dad shook each of their hands. "Have you three considered the Marines after high school? You have what it takes. You talk to a recruiter and need a reference, you give me a call."

"We might take you up on that," Raul answered. Nico and Angelo nodded and grinned agreement.

"And you three still have work in the morning. Even though I appreciate you ignoring my direct orders earlier. " A weary Reverend Yates finally managed to get the three teens headed home, then walked the rest of us out to where Dad's rental car was pulled up next to the reverend's in the rear parking lot.

"I'll be back to make arrangements to pay for the window," Dad told Reverend Yates.

"Not necessary. Insurance would cover it even if you hadn't broken it in the process of saving myself and these ladies." Reverend Yates turned to my birth mom. Someone, whether the reverend or a police officer, had administered First Aid to the cut on her cheekbone, and she'd sponged the blood from her shirt and tidied her hair. "Ashlyn, I know you took a cab here. Would you like me to drop you off somewhere?"

"No, she's coming with us. Then we'll get her home." Dad looked over at Ashlyn. "If that's okay with you, April. I know it's late, but I can't imagine any of us are going to sleep until we all get some answers."

It still felt odd for Dad to be calling her that. He turned to me. "Reese and I came straight here from the airport, but your mom will have us checked into a hotel by now."

He checked his phone. "Yep, she sent the address. A bit north of Central Park, so not far. Why don't we head there, order some room service, and fill each other in."

His glance my way was stern this time, and I swallowed hard. But I was so glad he was there I didn't care how much trouble I was in. How could I ever have doubted who my real parents were and how much Dad and Mom loved me, no matter what DNA said?

CHAPTER TWENTY-NINE

At Dad's firm orders, no one spilled their story until we got to the hotel. When we entered the hotel suite, there was another flurry of hugs and exclamations. That my parents had sprung for a two-bedroom-and-lounge-area suite on top of plane tickets told me more than anything how anxious they'd been to find me.

Mom seemed almost as happy to see Ashlyn as me, her misplaced daughter. By the time my two moms emerged from their hugs and tears, a lot of past misunderstandings appeared to have been erased. Reese put in a sizeable order to room service. While we waited for the food, Dad turned to me.

"Okay, Bailey, we've got a pretty good idea of your story up to this afternoon, thanks to Reese and Draya. But why don't you fill in the blanks. Then April and I can do the same."

"Actually, I go by Ashlyn now," Ashlyn spoke up. "And I don't really want to go back to the person April was."

"Okay, Ashlyn it is," Dad said.

"I'll tell my part," I agreed. "But first I want to know how you and Reese ended up here bursting into the church like that. Raul said they caught you casing the place. How could you possibly have known I was there?"

Dad nodded toward Reese. "That was your boyfriend here's doing."

My boyfriend again and this time from my dad? I liked the

sound of it but cast an embarrassed glance at Reese. He didn't seem bothered, and his responding smile was wide, so I smiled in return.

Reese spoke up. "I called your dad after Draya told me what was going on. I get why you didn't tell me, and I know you didn't want your parents finding out. But with Draya on a plane to Sri Lanka and you in a city like New York City all alone with a lowlife like Martin stalking you—well, I couldn't forgive myself if something happened to you. And whatever was going on between you and your parents—"

He broke off, suddenly looking embarrassed. "—I know what it's like to be angry with your parents but still know deep down they love you. And your parents are good folks. They needed to know you might be in danger. I figured I might take a bus here myself or even drive to get here quicker. But the instant I told your dad Martin might be after you, he insisted on booking the first flight he could get. Then once we got here—"

"You don't need to explain," I interrupted dryly. "I already got the point you finally showed my tech-allergic dad how to turn on the phone finder!"

I then told my own story, going back to seeing the Portraits of Summer exhibit in Chicago and how I'd met Martin. By the time I got to the events of this evening, Mom had paled considerably. When I finished, she walked over to put her arms around me.

Then Dad turned to Ashlyn. "Okay, your turn, sis. All these years we thought you were dead. There are no words to say how glad I am we were wrong. But where were you? We searched for you everywhere. Even hired private investigators."

Ashlyn looked down at her clasped hands for a long moment before she began telling the same story she'd told me. "If I'd ever dreamed Summer—Bailey—was still alive . . . but maybe it was just as well I didn't. Even after I got clean, I can't pretend she'd have been better off with me than with you. Reverend Yates helped me see God had a plan for me even after all I'd done. Even so, it took a couple more years before I really got my act together enough to hold a steady job."

She twisted her hands together, then looked at Dad. "That's when I went back to Chicago to look for you. I figured I at least owed it to you to let you know what I'd done to my baby. I knew how much you loved Summer. But you were gone, and I couldn't find you. Then my art took off—another miracle I never expected. After all God had done for me, I figured maybe I could make amends for all the hurt and trouble I'd caused by helping others find their way. So I started volunteering with the rehab program and youth center."

"Oh, honey!" Dad looked devastated at Ashlyn's story. "I'd give anything to change things. To have let you know Bailey was safe with us. If we'd known you were alive. Or that Martin was behind bars."

Ashlyn blinked hard, then brushed a hand across her eyelashes before asking, "So why did you take her? Why did you change your name? I know Patty could never have a baby, and for a brief minute when Summer—Bailey—told me what you'd done, I really did think you'd stolen her to get back at me for going back to Martin and taking Bailey away from you. But I simply couldn't believe it. Maybe I was that kind of person and Martin for sure. But not you two."

175

Dad sighed heavily. "It wasn't something I'd ever thought we'd do. Patty and I were so worried when we hadn't heard from you in weeks we finally drove over to the last address we had for you. We found Martin drinking. Bailey was wandering around crying with a cast on her arm, a full diaper, and so filthy you could hardly see her face. Martin told us you'd abandoned him and your baby and that he'd heard from a dealer pal you'd gotten into some bad heroin and overdosed."

"We didn't believe him," Mom put in. "Not without evidence. So we told Martin we'd take Bailey home and care for her until you came back. He simply laughed at us and grabbed her up so tightly she started screaming. He said if we didn't believe him just check the Jane Does. Then he said he'd already made arrangements for a private adoption, and unless we could top the current offer of a hundred thousand, we'd never see Bailey again."

"That's where I made a mistake," Dad interjected sadly. "I told him flat-out selling a baby was illegal and I'd call the police if he tried it. He went ballistic, screaming for us to get out of his house. He said he wouldn't consider an offer from us and as her father he'd make sure we'd never see Bailey again. And all the time she was screaming at the top of her lungs."

"It was her broken arm." Mom's face held an expression of remembered horror. "He was squeezing the cast against him, and I knew she had to be in terrible pain. I yelled at him to let her go or I'd call 911 to get Child Protective Services down there immediately.

Tears of memory were in Mom's eyes. "He laughed and said no social worker was going to take a motherless little girl away from her only living parent, and he was the one who would be calling the police on us if we didn't leave immediately. He practically dared me to call CPS. Said there'd be nothing to report by the time they arrived. Then he smelled her like he'd just noticed her dirty diaper and dropped her to the floor. She landed right on her cast, whimpering like she was barely conscious."

Dad looked over at me. "That's when we knew we couldn't leave you there another night, honey. Mom and I were both out of our minds with worry that in his state he'd end up killing you."

"So what did you do?" I asked. "Why didn't you call the police?"

Dad shook his head. "Because Martin was right. All he had to do was clean you up, feed you, and get you to stop crying. We had no legal leg to stand on, and anything CPS did find, he could blame on April. The broken arm was already on record as April's doing."

"That's why we went back," Mom said. "We knew drunk as he was he'd be passed out. And what he didn't know was that April had left behind her key to Martin's house along with a bunch of baby stuff we'd bought for you when she went back to him. We waited until well after midnight, then went in the back door. Sure enough, we could hear Martin snoring. You weren't even in your crib but lying on the living room floor still in that dirty diaper, no bottle around, and whimpering as though you were too far gone with pain and hunger and thirst to even cry anymore."

Dad picked up the story. "Your mom grabbed you up. Martin

must have heard something because he was suddenly out of bed and stumbling for us like an intoxicated two-ton grizzly. We got out of the house and into our car before he could stop stumbling long enough to catch us. But we didn't dare go home. Martin would never give up a hundred thousand dollars, and we knew there was nothing he'd like better than to tell the police we'd kidnapped his precious daughter.

"We did stop long enough to pack a couple suitcases, including our personal papers and photos and all the baby stuff we still had there. Then we got what we could of our savings at the nearest ATMs and headed toward a small Indiana town I'd visited when I was a child. It was as small and unnoticed as when I was a kid, and there was no one left who would know me."

Dad let out a sigh. "I waited for months, checking the news, expecting there would be an Amber Alert out on Bailey. When none ever showed, I assumed Martin had decided against calling the cops, maybe to keep from drawing attention to his own criminal activity. So I went back to Chicago and sold our home to one of those 'buy your house as is for cash' companies. We used the money to start our mechanic shop. And to purchase some fake IDs. You know the rest, Bailey, as you've lived it with us."

Tears flowed down Ashlyn's features, so much like mine and Dad's. Dad reached over and touched her hand tenderly.

"I'm sorry, April. Had I known you were looking for us, I'd have never disappeared like that. I did what Martin said and checked out the Jane Does, but none of them was you. And I continued searching for April Hill, hoping you might turn up somewhere. But you never did, so I came to believe Martin was right, and you had died somewhere but hadn't ended up in any system I could check. I hope you can understand—"

Ashlyn broke into his apology. "Understand? I'm more grateful than I can express. There's something I never told you. When I first got pregnant, Martin wanted me to get an abortion. When I said no, he kept talking about how a baby would ruin our lifestyle."

Ashlyn wiped an arm across her wet face. "Then suddenly when the ultrasound showed it was a girl, he stopped pushing for an abortion and started telling me how much money a baby girl was worth. How some people would pay a hundred thousand for a little girl. When I asked him who would pay that much, he shrugged and said there were childless couples who would spend that much or more for a private adoption. I even thought about it as I knew I wasn't ready to be a mother, though that seemed a lot of money for a legit adoption. Then later I found his laptop open to information about high-paying illegal adoptions, and I didn't know if our little girl would be going to a childless couple or be sold for something much worse."

Ashlyn's glance went from Dad to Mom. "That's why I moved back in with you guys for the rest of my pregnancy and after. I didn't want to tell you what Martin had wanted to do. I still loved him. Or thought I did. More so, I think I loved the freedom and lifestyle he gave me."

She hunched her shoulders in misery. "Martin told you the truth on the rest. I was a terrible mother, especially when he got me back on drugs. It was my fault Summer broke her arm, so I really believed him when he told me I'd killed my baby."

Ashlyn looked squarely at Dad. "When I came to live with you after my mom died, I thought you were ruining my life. All those rules and regulations. And I was just as bad when you were trying to help me after Bailey was born. But I was the one who ruined my own life. And almost ruined my daughter's."

She looked over at Mom. "Thank you for loving my baby in my place."

Then she turned her saddened gaze to me. "I was such a mess. I hurt you. I abandoned you without even trying to find out if Martin was really telling the truth. All the lies he told, I should have guessed he might be lying then. But I was never sober enough to have my head clear for a good couple years after that. If I hadn't come across Reverend Yates, I'm sure I would have been dead of an overdose as Martin claimed."

I took a deep breath, not sure if I could speak without choking up with emotion. Things were finally falling into place. I managed to get the words out. "You didn't get to raise me, but Mom and Dad did. I've been safe and loved all these years."

The only thing that saved us from a flood of emotions was Dad's phone ringing just then. Looking at the Caller ID, he rose to his feet, walked into the suite's bathroom, and closed the door. The rest of us sat in silence, listening to the occasional "uh-huh" and murmuring behind the door.

When Dad emerged, he had a satisfied look on his face. "Well, that was an interesting conversation. You aren't going to believe—"

"Tell us!" I said. "Is it about Martin?"

"That was the lead detective on the case. Seems Martin is back to prison since possession of an illegal firearm, threatening civilians, and taking a reverend hostage are all serious parole violations. So we won't have to worry about him again for another decade or so."

Dad's expression turned suddenly serious. "Beyond that, I'd asked the detective to do some digging for me. It always puzzled me Martin never even tried to come after us. Turns out the DEA had their eyes on Martin, and the very day after we took Bailey, they raided his operation. Except his name was never Martin Beck. It was Richard Martin. Under that name, he had a rap sheet for drug-dealing and arrest warrants as long as my arm. He'd changed his name when he moved to Chicago to get a fresh start. He was charged with intent to distribute under his real name, took a plea deal, and went to prison. That's why I could never track him down. He was released a month ago and began looking for us and April—not to find his family but to get the drug stash he'd hidden away so he could start over. The funny thing is—"

He looked at Ashlyn. "Not funny ha-ha but ironic. The DEA's canine unit smelled out his stash walled up inside what was Bailey's nursery back then. The wall was ripped out, and the drugs went into evidence. Since Martin took a plea deal, they didn't have to turn over all the evidence they'd recovered, so he never knew it was gone. Especially since the house was repaired and sold at a government seized-goods auction. Which is why neither of you found any evidence of the other when you went back."

Dad let out a long, contented sigh. "The good news is that no one's looking to press charges for our having taken Bailey. Seems Ashlyn here told the police how grateful she was that her brother and sister-in-law had taken custody of her daughter since she hadn't been fit to care for a child. She also explained that our change of identity was necessary because Martin was a dangerous criminal who would have harmed her child and the child's new parents if he'd found them. Since it isn't actually illegal to change your name, the police have no interest in following up further in what the detective dismissed as a 'family matter'."

"It was the least I could do," Ashlyn said simply. "You and Patty were far better parents than I could have been. Just as you were to me. And with your nurture and upbringing, I have faith Bailey will never make the mistakes I did."

Dad looked around at the entire group. "So the question now is where we go from here. The detective asked us to stay in town another day since there are still some details he wants explained. Then we fly home. April—Ashlyn, if I ever remember to call you that—you are welcome to come with us."

Ashlyn was shaking her head. "No, New York City is now my home. I have a new art show to finish and responsibilities at the church and gallery. Bailey is your daughter and always will be. If I'm a different person than the nineteen-year-old who ran away from Chicago, she is a different, all-grown-up person than the baby I missed so desperately all these years. But I'd love to have her visit me here so we can get to know each other."

She gave me a tremulous smile. "I know it's a bit late to even try being a mother. But maybe we can be friends, and next time you come to New York City I can show you my favorite places."

I walked over and gave her a fierce hug, then wrapped an arm around Mom, who was sitting next to Ashlyn. "I would love that. As to being a mother—" I gave my mom a look that held all the love that was in me. She nodded slightly. "—I think Mom and I both agree there is plenty of love to go around in this family for two mothers."

Ashlyn and Mom looked at each other, tears threatening to spill over. It took room service arriving with our late meal to restore enough emotional equilibrium to enjoy our food. But by the end, Dad was himself enough to make corny jokes while Mom and Ashlyn were chatting together like sisters. I curled up on the couch next to Reese, whose arm around my shoulders seem to confirm those comments of being my boyfriend, even though previously Dad had insisted we would have to wait until I was older to date.

Today I felt older. So much had happened it was hard to believe only a few weeks had passed since the morning I'd been sneaking around in my parents' home office. I'd had a crash course in maturity. Being together with my whole family and Reese at my side seemed natural.

The feeling remained the next morning as we met the head detective back at the church and filled in all the details of our past history with Martin. Dad and Mom had decided to do a legal name change since April was keeping her own new name and everyone in our hometown knew us as the Collins family.

Another bit of good news for my parents was that Dad could finally draw on his military pension. This had built up in the bank where it had been automatically deposited for the past thirteen years. I felt better about the airplane tickets and hotel stay once I found out.

I still felt guilty for everything I'd put them through and the things I'd imagined when all the time they'd simply been protecting me. That said, I couldn't be sorry. Not with the way everything had turned out. Getting to meet my birth mom. Ashlyn getting to find out she hadn't killed her baby. Martin back in jail. A healed relationship between my parents and Dad's little sister.

The detective finally released us all, and we headed into the church to say goodbye to Reverend Yates. I wanted to say goodbye to my three teen rescuers, but they were all back to their daily lives and jobs. So I recorded a voice message on Reverend Yates's cell-phone to thank them.

We had flights early the next morning, and Ashlyn had an evening event with her new exhibit, so we said our goodbyes to Ashlyn before leaving the church. She'd already promised to fly out for a week before the end of summer—and to give me some tips on improving my own photography.

As Mom, Dad, and Reese headed across the basketball court to where our rental car was parked outside the mesh fencing, Ashlyn and I lagged behind and walked over to the wall mural. I reached up a finger and touched a colorful whorl on the "Created" art.

"It's hard to believe I didn't even know you existed until a few weeks ago. If you hadn't painted this, I'd never have found you. It's so beautiful. I'm still amazed what an incredible artist you are."

"Thanks to God's redemption and Reverend Yates's patience," Ashlyn responded. "From what I hear, you're a pretty good photographer yourself. If I hadn't created that Summer exhibit as a tribute to my lost child and if you hadn't been interested in photography enough to go all the way to Chicago to see it, I'd never have found you either. Maybe someday we can do an exhibit together—'Families.'"

She turned from the mural to smile at me. "You've been more forgiving of me than I ever was of my own mom when she was still alive. She wasn't much of a mother, but I was a pretty rotten daughter too. I'd give anything to go back and do it all differently. But if I'd raised you, I don't think you'd be the incredible person you are now. I'm looking forward to getting to know you."

I felt my face grow red, embarrassed at the praise. "I'm looking forward to getting to know you too. You've found your purpose, and I'm not sure about mine."

"Choose to believe you were created as a masterpiece even when you don't feel like it. And believe God has something special planned for you— because he does, and I can't wait to see where it leads. I'm so thankful I'll be a part of it."

"Me too," I said. "I wish it wasn't so long until you come to visit. But I'm a little glad to be heading home, even if I'll be lucky not to be grounded until I go to college. But at least now I know the truth about who I am and where I belong. I belong in Indiana with my parents, and I belong here, but most of all I belong to God, and that will lead me the right way."

As Ashlyn and I turned away from the mural, I saw that my parents and Reese had stopped in the middle of the basketball court to wait for us. A lightbulb went off in my head, and I dug into my ever-present camera bag to pull out my camera. "Reese, would you do me a favor? Before we go, I'd like a picture with all of my parents."

Mom, Dad, Ashlyn, and I posed in front of the mural, making sure the "Created" and "In Christ Jesus" wording was visible. It was a photo I knew I'd always cherish as it portrayed the way all the pieces of my life had finally come together. I couldn't wait to share this story with Draya. She was never going to believe all she'd missed, but I had the feeling there were many more adventures ahead.

About the author:

Kathy Cassel is author of more a dozen fiction and non-fiction titles for preteens and teens with Tyndale House Publishers and Legacy Press. Her Christian Girls Guide series won an iParenting award, and her first teen novel *Freerunner* was a 2021 Selah Award finalist. Kathy is passionate about writing realistic issues-based YA/teen fiction that not only entertains but also offers hope and healing. To better relate to her characters, she enjoys learning their skills such as whitewater rafting, scuba diving, and riding a motorcycle, but draws the line at sky diving.

Kathy has a B.S. degree in elementary education from Grace College, Winona Lake, Indiana, and a M.Ed. with a reading specialty. She grew up in northern Indiana, lived in three different continents while her husband was in the USAF, and now lives in the Florida Panhandle, all of which impacts the wide range of her fictional settings and characters. She and her husband have eight children, five of whom are adopted, three from Haiti and two from the United States. They also have six grandchildren. Kathy's favorite activities are those that involve traveling and adventures that include her children and grandchildren.

Don't Miss
Freerunner
by Kathy Cassel

Chapter One

Night is my favorite time of day. Night's when I can be anonymous, swallowed by darkness, when I run to outdistance the voices in my head and the images that are never far away.

As I stretch out on my quilt-covered bed, memories haunt me. I can't shut them off. I text my best friend Thorn, a high school freshman like me. Then, as I've done so many nights, I swing a leg, then the other, over my windowsill and slide onto the porch roof, careful to avoid the places that need repair. The noxious smell of the paper mill three miles away assaults my nose. It's stronger than usual tonight.

It's mid-February, and, while it's not cold in the Florida Panhandle, the air is a bit chilly now the sun's gone down. A breeze blows a wisp of thick, dark hair into my face. I brush it aside and stride to the roof's edge, jump, and front-flip midair. Landing in a crouch, I roll to break my fall. It's no problem for me. Just another bit of freerunning. And that's what I do best.

I pull my phone from my pocket and text: "Meet me at the playground."

My phone buzzes, and I read the one-word answer. "Now?"

"It's important."

Almost instantly, the phone vibrates again. "On my way."

I stick my phone in my pocket, then jog down the street to the elementary school playground where I first saw freerunning in action—a group of older boys racing around the playground, going over, instead of around, the benches and play equipment.

The combination of gymnastic and acrobatic moves, creative yet intentional, had intrigued me. Soon I was trying to copy them, laying claim to that same playground. Stairs with a center railing lead up to the school, high on a hill above the playground. I jog up those stairs, staying to the right of the railing. At the top, I turn and peer into the darkness below.

A lone streetlight casts a glow on the playground. The other lights were broken long ago and never replaced. The play area is a large asphalt square, surrounded by fields on two sides. The hill where I'm standing makes up the third side. A road runs beside the playground and dead ends into a rusty chain-link fence behind a convenience store on the fourth side. The store owners put up the fence to keep kids from going onto their property, but it's in bad shape and does little to keep anyone away.

How long before Thorn gets here? I need to talk to him, to tell him the news I received earlier that made my world tilt. I gaze around, but there's only the four netless basketball hoops perched on posts, like sentinels guarding the old-fashioned play equipment. No Thorn yet.

The images start to come, the same ones that have haunted me for years. A young girl celebrating her sixth birthday. Twirling round and round in a new pink party dress and white sandals with straps that wrap around her ankles. Feeling like a princess.

I know what's coming next, so I jump to my feet and race down the stairs, vaulting back and forth across the center railing until I reach the playground. Trying to escape the pictures playing in my mind, I cross the asphalt and run toward a bench, planting my hand on the back and bringing both legs over for a speed vault.

The swings, bars, slides, and merry-go-round in front of me are well-worn and a bit rusty, but they hold the memories of thousands of children over the years. This equipment is clustered around a newer wooden playset made up of ladders, bridges, slides, and climbing bars that work well for the jumps, flips, and vaults that make up freerunning.

The dim glow of the streetlight illuminates Thorn as he approaches the playground. He's wearing long cotton pajama bottoms, a black tank top, and high-top basketball shoes, same as me, but my shoes are black and white and held together with silver duct tape.

The slight chill of the night air doesn't bother us. We stay warm freerunning. I stride along the border of the playground near Thorn. He falls in beside me and matches his stride to mine. He has his own issues to deal with, so he gets it when I need to run away from the memories that haunt me. Most nights we run in silence in our own version of follow-the-leader.

Passing me, Thorn heads toward a brick wall meant to close off the corner of the playground housing the dumpster and storage shed. It doesn't accomplish that task but gives us a good wall for stunts. Planting his foot hip-high against the wall, Thorn pushes upward off the bricks and performs a perfect back flip. I follow, but back flips are tricky for me. I plant my foot wrong when I push off, sending me downward instead of into the air. I land hard on my bottom.

Thorn drops beside me. "Interesting move."

"Yeah, needs a little work."

"You forgot to drive your knee upward."

I snort. "Obviously."

My mood darkens as I remember why I wanted to talk to him.

Thorn lifts an eyebrow. "What?"

"He called. Mom talked to him."

"Kia ..."

My heart lightens at Thorn's nickname for me. To everyone else, I'm Kiana Scott, but to Thorn, I'm just Kia. Like the car.

"He called," I repeat. "Just like that. Like he has a right." By saying the words aloud, I'm acknowledging it to myself. The *he* isn't my dad, because I don't know who my father is. It's the other he. The one who ruined me—Mom's father.

I jump up and take off, circling the playground with long, strong strides, trying unsuccessfully to slam the door of my mind on the thought of him. Thorn follows me as I weave in and out of the basketball poles, swinging myself in a wide arc on each pole.

I race to the horizontal bars, swing up, and sit. Thorn lands beside me, sweat glistening on his skin. Our arms touch, his white, mine light brown. Thorn calls me dusky.

He tilts his head to the side, studying me. "What does he want?"

I scoot to the edge of the bars and swing my legs back and forth. "Has cancer." I say it fast to cover the tremor in my voice. "Says he wants Mom's support."

"Really?" Thorn tightens his lips, then speaks again. "Her support?"

"So he says." I reach in my pocket and feel the Statue of Liberty souvenir coin my third-grade teacher gave me for getting a 100% on my geography test. I've carried it with me since. Prizes are rare in my world. I rub the coin between my thumb and first finger.

Thorn's eyes narrow. "He expects your mom to do what?"

"Don't know. But now, I'm thinking of what he did all over again." I release the coin and rub the back of my neck.

Thorn gives a quiet laugh. Not the kind that means something's funny ... the other kind. "Like you ever stopped. Like you even could."

I swing my legs harder. "I try."

He turns toward me. "You run."

I shrug one shoulder. "It's what I do best. Run."

Thorn's face is only inches from mine, his warm breath tickling my cheek. "Maybe it's time you face the issue."

If only it were that easy. If only bile didn't rise in my throat thinking about it. "It's too late. It can't be undone. I'll never be a normal teen. Normal was stolen from me."

Thorn looks thoughtful. He runs his hand backward through his closely clipped dark-blonde hair. What can he say? I'm right.

"True ..."

"But?"

"There's always hope."

"Hope for what?"

"A new ending. You can't change the beginning, but you don't have to let him write the ending too."

At Thorn's words, I feel a spark of some emotion I can't name. I don't know what to do or say, so I jump from the bars and cross the playground to the road home. Thorn is behind me as I jog down the street. Two dogs have tipped over a trashcan and are scavenging through the contents. The stench of rotted food invades my senses, making the inside of my nose burn. I speed up, and Thorn keeps pace. We race to my house where I grasp the cool metal porch post and pull myself up, hand over hand, my muscles taut.

I reach the roof. My fingertips grasp the edge. I pull myself up, ignoring the pain as rough shingles bite into my skin. Thorn is right behind me. We sit side by side next to my bedroom window, leaning against the house. My skin prickles from the cool aluminum siding. My tank top isn't warm enough now that we've stopped running, but

I'm not ready to go inside yet.

The clouds part, and points of light blaze above us. Why does the night sky make me long for something I can't even name? I gaze upward and point. "There's Orion. See the three stars in a row? That's his belt."

I glance at Thorn. He's motionless, knees to his chest, arms wrapped loosely around them. His lips are slightly parted, and he gazes upward.

From down the street, a child's cry is followed by yelling and the crash of shattering glass, breaking the spell cast by the expanse of stars. Just another night on Willow Street, a place where people dump their junk curbside until the next pick-up day, so a constant assortment of old tires, appliances, and bathroom fixtures adorn the roadside the way trees and flowers do in other sections of town. A sigh escapes my lips. My surroundings are a reminder that my life has too much debris and not enough flowers.

Thorn turns to me, a question in his eyes.

I take a breath and blow it out slowly. "Why'd he have to call? Isn't it enough that I relive his abuse over and over in my dreams?"

I pull my knees to my chest and clutch them tightly until they start to cramp. I release my grip and stretch my legs. There's another tear in my shoe. I need more duct tape, my solution to most things in my life. But duct tape can't fix everything.

"Maybe he's got regrets," Thorn says.

I don't turn to face him, but I know he's watching me. I can feel it. I huff, air escaping from my nostrils. "Regrets for what he did to me? Not likely. Shouldn't make a difference to me anyway. I'm not six anymore."

"If it didn't make a difference, the memories wouldn't still haunt you."

I pull my legs to my chest and lean forward. "You know what it's like to hide something. To pretend it never happened. My grandfather. Your dad." I turn my head to look at him. "You and me? We both come from a hard place."

Thorn shifts sideways, looking directly at me. "Doesn't change the fact there's a plan for us. Someone bigger than us is orchestrating things."

Thorn's face is illuminated by the stars and a dim streetlight. I look into his shadowed blue eyes, searching my face. I open my mouth, trying to form an answer. This isn't the first time we've had this conversation.

"If there is a God, how could he sit back and watch what my grandfather did to me? What your dad did to you and your mom? What kind of God would let little kids get hurt?"

Thorn looks down and shakes his head. "I don't know the answer to that. But I know I trust him, look to him for courage, for the strength to do what it takes to make things change. Maybe it's time you claim the courage to do what you need to do."

I press my lips together, then exhale. "Like what? Have a chat with my grandfather? Tell him I forgive him for what he did? No thanks."

"No. Not that. But maybe you're meant to finally face it. Start writing your new ending."

I breathe in slowly through my nose and out my mouth. "Why now? I don't even know where to begin."

He turns his head to look at me. "Why not now? Don't let him win."

Heat rushes through me. Thorn doesn't get it. My grandfather has already won. "I can't talk about this more. I need to sleep."

I stand. Thorn looks up at me, but for now the conversation is over. I turn and slip through the open window into my room, then look back and watch as Thorn walks to the edge of the roof. He drops from view, and I hear a soft thud. His shadow disappears into the night.

Don't Miss
Catching Hope
by Kathy Cassel

Chapter One

The sound of a horn startled me awake. I struggled to a sitting position, excitement pulsing through me. I was in a large van sitting between my sixteen-year-old adoptive brother, Chad, and Levi, my twin, who were both still asleep. I nudged Levi until he opened his eyes and sat up. His red hair, a shade darker than mine, was tousled, and his sapphire blue eyes were sleepy. It had been a long drive from the airport to our resort on the Haitian coastline, and although I'd wanted to stay awake and take in the scenery, I drifted off.

Now we were stopped outside an ornate iron gate. Juvens, our driver, honked again, and a man in a uniform pushed a button triggering a motor to open the gate, allowing Juvens to pull through.

I turned to Levi. "Can you believe it? Us in a foreign country?"

He nodded but was silent. Handling new situations and the stress of unfamiliar places is hard for my twin. Until a year ago, Levi and I were bounced from foster home to foster home, never getting a forever family partly because Levi does things that make him stand out as different. The Michaels call it quirks of his autism, but other families weren't so understanding. In fact, they could be downright mean at times.

Right after our fourteenth birthday, our case manager moved Levi to a group home to help him transition into successful adult life. What really happened was he was targeted and ended up in the emergency room, where he first met Dr. Michaels. I met Dr. Michaels during the investigation into Levi's abuse. Then the Michaels decided to add us to their family.

After many discussions, accelerated training classes, and tons of paperwork, we were adopted. Dr. and Mrs. Michaels became our parents, and in the deal, we got a brother—Chad. He was adopted by the Michaels when he was six. Now he's sixteen, a year older than us. His skin is the color of caramel, and he's strong from all the sports he plays.

Our cousin Jen was in the seat in front of me next to Mrs. M. Jen is almost seventeen. Dr. Michaels and her dad, also known as Dr. Michaels, are brothers. She isn't adopted, and she let us know the first time we met. Thankfully, she lives in Michigan, and we live in the Florida panhandle, so it's not like we hang out much.

Even after the flight from Miami and the long van ride, her blond hair was pulled up in a perfect top knot. I made a mental note to ask Mrs. M to help me do something with my wild tangle of red hair once we were settled in.

Jen scowled. "I don't know why I had to come on this trip. I would have been fine staying home alone while my parents went on their trip to Europe—their vacation which didn't include their only child."

Dr. M turned from the front passenger seat. "You'll have to take that up with your parents. They evidently wanted to spend time alone. And they thought this trip would be a good experience for you." He smiled.

Jen didn't return his smile. She stuck her earphones back into her ears, seemingly not as curious about our new accommodations as I was.

Juvens drove slowly through the resort. Small, white houses with yellow trim and blue shutters were set among palm trees. In the middle of the resort, four small swimming pools were situated around a central concrete island filled with dirt. Lush palm trees were planted in the ornamental island.

"This is where we're staying? In one of those little houses?" I could hear the wonder in my voice, and Jen didn't miss it even with headphones in.

"Bungalows," she said. "Not little houses."

"Little houses. Bungalows. Same thing," Chad said. "Who cares anyway? Look at the sea."

I followed Chad's gaze. Waves were rolling in and crashing onto a white sand beach, stretching as far as I could see. Chad's eyes devoured the water. "I can't wait to try out those waves!"

Juvens pulled in front of a bungalow, climbed out, and walked to the back of the van. He opened the back doors where our luggage was stored. As I went to get my luggage, a movement outside the fence drew my gaze. A short, thin man with skin like dark chocolate, a white scar etched above his right eye, was watching us. He focused on Dr. M, and his eyes narrowed, a look of pure hatred filling his face. His eyes met mine, and the look of fury on his face made my heart race. I quickly turned away. Who was the man? And more importantly, why was he looking at us as though he hated us?

FREERUNNER

A young adult novel by
Kathy Cassel

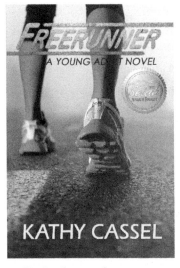

Night is Kia's favorite time, when she freeruns to outdistance the memories of abuse she suffered as a young child. But when former reality television star Terrence Jones arrives at their school as the new head track coach, things begin to change in unpredictable ways. Kia tries out for the team to fit in, but just as she's gaining a new sense of normal, her abuser steps back into her life. Not only that, but trouble between team members and coaches cause even more turmoil. Kia soon realizes she has to choose between running from her past or saving a child from the same sort of abuse she suffered. But will she have the courage to do so?